Freeway : La Movie

Freeway: La Movie

Jorge Enrique Lage

Translated from the Spanish by Lourdes Molina

DEEP VELLUM PUBLISHING

DALLAS, TEXAS

Deep Vellum Publishing
3000 Commerce St., Dallas, Texas 75226
deepvellum.org · @deepvellum

Deep Vellum is a 501c3 nonprofit literary arts organization
founded in 2013 with the mission to bring
the world into conversation through literature.

First US Edition, 2022

LIBRARY OF CONGRESS CATALOGING-IN-PUBLICATION DATA
Names: Lage, Jorge Enrique, 1979- author. | Molina, Lourdes, 1978- translator.
Title: Freeway : la movie / Jorge Enrique Lage ; translated from the Spanish by Lourdes Molina.
Other titles: Autopista. English
Description: First US edition. | Dallas, Texas : Deep Vellum Publishing, 2022.
Identifiers: LCCN 2022018608 | ISBN 9781646051823 (trade paperback) | ISBN 9781646051830 (ebook)
Subjects: LCGFT: Satirical literature. | Dystopian fiction. | Linked stories.
Classification: LCC PQ7392.L34 A9613 2022 | DDC 863/.7--dc23/eng/20220418
LC record available at https://lccn.loc.gov/2022018608

ISBN (TPB) 978-1-64605-182-3
ISBN (Ebook) 978-1-64605-183-0

Exterior design by Emily Mahon
Interior layout and typesetting by KGT

PRINTED IN THE UNITED STATES OF AMERICA

CONTENTS

Las Breaking News

She doesn't mean anything to me, yet I will pursue the mystery of her death.

RODOLFO WALSH

They say the Freeway is going to cut through the city, from top to bottom. What's left of the city, anyway. During the day, bulldozers sweep through parks, buildings, shopping centers. At night, I wander by the sea, through the debris, the machines, the shipping containers, trying to imagine the magnitude of what's to come. There's no doubt the Freeway is going to be monstrous.

•

That's the thing about freeways: no matter where they go, the desert begins to grow on either side. Sprawling, spreading like weeds from outer space and consuming all possibilities, el desierto.

•

Tonight, I ran into him again. I call him "El Autista." At one point, he was some sort of nerd, a geek, a freak. He seems beyond all that now. I found him in a car graveyard, by an exhibit of classic American-made bodies that have to be more than a century old by now. Sitting silently under a tangle of multicolored cables and wires he spliced together, he reads the latest issue of *Wired*. I nod and keep going. Someone should really make a documentary about him.

A shipping container. Mysteriously open. I light a match and shine it on the metal door. A bunch of stickers: SNACK CULTURE. On the outside, on both sides, in even bigger letters, it probably says the same thing: SNACK CULTURE. Inside there is (there has to be) a corpse.

•

"Anything else?" asks El Autista.

"Boxes, boxes, boxes."

"I mean, are there any other bodies?"

"Just you and me."

"Other bodies. Other bodies."

He's practically begging me for bodies. I ask him:

"Why would there be any other bodies?"

A fleet of helicopters flies across the moon. When they disappear, El Autista turns to me. With a blank stare, he says:

"It's always the same thing: you, me, and a dead woman."

•

Dressed like a queen—more like a puta dressed as a queen—in an evening gown, stilettos, and a Louis Vuitton bag. A high-end pool of blood beneath her. She dressed up to go out with someone. Was it dinner? A red-carpet event? A party? Something went wrong. Hair undone. Perfect makeup. Well over forty, she's not a young woman but bears the (surgically crafted) features of one. She wears jewels but has no money. There's no doubt she must have had lots of friends and countless lovers. One could conjure all kinds of sordid stories just by looking at her sprawled across the container floor. She is, of course, Vida Guerra. The cubano-americana model, singer, actress. Even now, her face is unmistakable.

•

We have to do something. I suggest we look for a phone. We need to find a damn cell phone. Let's go to Nokia, that small town in Finland, and stay there forever.

But we don't move. We wonder if one of us should stay behind watching (maybe carefully examining) Vida's corpse. It starts to drizzle in the middle of our necrophilic discussion. We hadn't noticed the light rain approaching us.

For an instant, as it brushes up against our noses, we see this:

What first looked like a veil of water turns out to be more like a front of electronic ether. Like a screen filled with static. Like glass that turns everything on the other side into liquid. It passes over us. It doesn't provoke any sensations, and everything remains as it was before. Yet, everything is now somehow in grayscale and brighter.

El Autista and I look at each other.

El Autista tells me he knows where he can find a stretcher.

I think to myself: That hospital dumpster only exists in his mind.

We place the dead cubano-americana on the metal stretcher and wheel it to the area's watchtower.

The watchman comes out and shines his flashlight at us:

"Stop! Who are you?"

We don't respond. Theory of reflexive silence.

But seriously, who *are* we?

"How did you get in here?"

"We were always in here," El Autista says.

"What do you have there?" The watchman comes closer and inspects the stretcher. "People come here to steal construction materials, but instead you . . ."

"Sir, do you recognize who this is?" I ask. "Look closely."

He squints. He's fat, pathetic, about ten battered years older than Vida and—at the very least—seems to need a pair of glasses.

"This is a fine cougar," he acknowledges. "You can tell she's a spicy devil. I have a heart condition because of hot little numbers like this."

"You can find a list of transplants in heart magazines,"

El Autista tells him for no particular reason. "One must read everything."

The watchman looks at El Autista carefully.

"I'm on a transplant list, you know."

"Then what are you doing here?" I ask.

"I'm waiting for them to finish the Freeway. They pay shit, but at least they pay. I was a colonel in las Fuerzas Armadas, you know, and look where I've ended up: in a watchtower watching TV all night." El Coronel looks at the corpse. He snaps his fingers. "I know! She's the lady from the news."

We go inside the watchtower. *El Noticiero Nacional* is on a portable black-and-white TV, and there she is. Live and alive. Vida Guerra is the main female anchor. With a killer neckline, she reports on a tidal wave in Asia. Then she appears as the main male anchor. Vida Guerra with a thick mustache, her hair hidden under a wig, her breasts compressed under a suit and tie. She's also the weatherwoman in another outfit: different fitted pants, but the same voice. She runs her hands over the map of the Island, revealing (provoking) high temperatures. Following this, Vida Guerra is the handsome young sports reporter who chats with the gray-haired baseball analyst, who is also her. And then, Vida Guerra with the culture report: chubby-cheeked, a homely smile, a plain shirt. Finally, Vida Guerra reporting on Vida Guerra, the correspondent who reports from all over the world. Go ahead, Vida. Thank you very much.

•

"This has to mean something," El Coronel says, as his eyes widen and his skin turns pale. He has seen a clear sign revealed in the superimposed images of the body we just found. Without a doubt, all this has to do with him; it all points in that direction. He was waiting for her, and she finally found him. The fatal hour has come. (But something else occurs to me.)

•

"Maybe it's not what you think," I suggest. "Sir, without trying to invalidate your conjecture, and with the utmost respect, I think it may be just the opposite: This may be your opportunity to get a new heart."

Puzzled, El Coronel blinks.

"Her heart? Take *her* heart?"

"Right now, before it gets cold. If what you say is true, you have nothing to lose. On the contrary, if everything goes well . . ."

"But how could I possibly live with a woman's heart?!"

"If a woman can, Coronel, you can, too."

He stands in silence. Pensively, he brings his hand to his chest and taps it.

El Autista and I look at each other.

El Autista tells me he knows where he can find a stretcher.

I think:

•

He wouldn't dare. I'm sure of it. Yet, without hesitation, El Coronel lies down on the metal stretcher next to Vida. He closes his eyes and appears determined, more than determined: anesthetized.

"Scalpel," I prompt El Autista.

I stare at the donor and try to concentrate.

I tear the fabric of her dress. She's not wearing a bra, of course.

I move her left breast out of the way. If I cut the wrong spot, a stream of silicone may squirt out. Maybe I'll find a stray bullet. A wad of dollars. Anything could happen.

I make the incision. I open the flesh. I go in. I pull the ribs away from the plastic. I push everything aside that isn't important right now.

The heart comes into view. I cut the tubing and cables attached to it. I stick my dirty hands into her chest, which is still warm and only getting warmer . . .

It burns.

(A puff of scented smoke.)

I remove Vida Guerra's heart.

"That's gross," El Autista says behind me.

I hold Vida Guerra's heart as if it were the most fragile thing in the world. It's moist. It's small and feminine. It's an erotic toy. Battery-powered, it vibrates in my hands. Or maybe my hands are vibrating, my nerves charging the heart with electricity.

All of a sudden, the heart beats. Only one beat. A strong beat.

I turn to El Autista.

“Did you see that?”

“No.”

I watch the heart for a few seconds. It doesn’t beat again. I squeeze it a bit. Nothing. I ask El Autista to hold it. I grab the scalpel.

“Don’t drop it. Give it to me when I ask for it.”

“Why would I want to keep it? She doesn’t mean anything to me.”

“Right.” I approach the other body. He’s already taken off his uniform shirt. His saggy, sunken chest has a few scattered hairs that look like writhing worms. I feel a heart, mine, beating hard. I look at El Autista. I look at the heart—that woman’s part in his hand. I look at the chest that has yet to be cut open. I pick up the scalpel. I let it fall.

I step back.

“I’m sorry, Coronel.”

He gets up. He starts to button up his shirt.

“I knew you wouldn’t dare,” he says.

Or would I?

Without hesitation, El Coronel lies on the metal stretcher next to Vida. He closes his eyes and appears determined, more than determined: anesthetized.

"Scalpel," I prompt El Autista.

1. I open her chest. I take out her heart.
2. I open his chest. I take out his heart.

I throw heart #2 in the trash. I place heart #1 inside him.

I close his chest while El Autista closes hers, murmuring:

"She doesn't mean anything to me, yet here I am, filling this hole with Freeway construction sand. She doesn't mean anything to me, yet here I am, sewing her ragged body with wire."

I ask him to be quiet because, at the end of the day, he's the only one who understands what he's trying to say. This is one of the reasons I call him "El Autista."

The military operation concludes at last.

"All set, Coronel."

He gets up. He starts buttoning up his shirt.

"Now let's bury that bitch," he says.

•

We no longer have to call the police: he's the police now. He tells us about the other bodies buried here. There's this place he knows about where people go (the guys who don't pay shit, the ones who actually pay) to get rid of bodies in the middle of the night. Vagrants. Hookers.

Onlookers. Bodies they toss from helicopters. And desperate fugitives who bury themselves, digging with their nails. Bodies nobody will ever find, El Coronel assures us. All of this will soon be buried under tons of asphalt as far as the eye can see. All of it.

•

The three of us walk in silence as we steer Vida's stretcher through paths of rocky terrain. We walk between trucks with huge tires. We edge around massive deposits of water and cement. Then the view broadens and reveals what is far beyond: the images of some satellite, the future maps of Google. I think about the infinite lanes of traffic that begin on the nearby continent, the infinity of bright lights, the horror of concrete, already crashing through the tropical waters, that will soon cut through this strip of deserted land to continue its way south, back to the sea.

•

El Coronel looks through the bushes and underneath boards. A pick and shovel appear in the moonlight. That's what we needed to cover up the transplant. The real and definitive proof of the transplant.

El Coronel shows me his chest. The scar is a red, swollen furrow with barbed wire stitched across it, ready to burst.

"This shoddy mess isn't proof enough?"

"No," I tell him. I know I'm right.

"Cállate. Let's dig this pit."

We dig. El Coronel digs with passion, with pride, with abandon, with brutality. He unleashes an energy that is out of this world.

•

We stop at an acceptable depth. El Coronel carries Vida Guerra and lays her down at the edge of the pit.

"Does anybody want to say a few words?"

I shrug my shoulders. I don't even know who she is. It's best to come up with a theory. Or to contradict one. But I don't say anything.

(Vida's Life: from La Habana to New Jersey, to the puffy eyes of the show, to the speed of classic cars that never stop, and back to La Habana once again and forever and . . .)

El Autista, as if he didn't want anybody else to hear, says:

"And nobody will ever know where to find you, Vida Google."

"Guerra," I correct him in vain.

El Coronel raises his hand:

"I do have a few words. What I have to say is the following," he says as he undoes his belt, opens his fly, and drops his pants and torn underwear. He lifts Vida's dress, rips off her lace panties and throws them into the pit. "Even though she's dead, this bitch is going to know what it's like to be with a macho cubano."

El Coronel strokes himself, trying to get an erection.

"I don't think this is the time," I tell him. El Autista taps my shoulder and hands me a magazine. It's the *Playboy* issue with Vida on the cover and centerfold. I really don't know where he finds these things.

"You'll see. You'll see . . ." Kneeling uncomfortably between Vida's open legs, El Coronel gropes her sutured chest. He sucks her bloody nipples. He fingers her while shaking his penis. He stretches it out. He grips it . . .

He can't get it up.

I leaf through the *Playboy*.

The reports, the interviews, the fiction . . .

I think about all the places where these sticky pages might have been read (and how they might have been read, and how many hands . . .). Offices. Garages. Basements. Farmlands lost amid a remote highway. Watchtowers along a path of ruins. This magazine has been traveling for a while, from hand to hand, a long way to El Autista, to me. It's an old issue, an issue from several years ago.

"Let's go, Coronel," I look up and watch him. The moment came and went.

"No, no . . . yes, I can . . . now . . ." He continues to masturbate without technique, without pause, without ever achieving a decent erection. "She's going to know I can have her just like anybody else," and with his hands shaking, he presses his wet glans to her dead labia, trying to find a way in. "I have her heart, but I'm still . . . I'm still me . . . right?" He looks at me, he looks at us. "Right?"

El Coronel breathes with difficulty. He suddenly stops fondling his crotch and starts pounding his chest. His face, covered in sweat, is frozen in a grimace. A cry of pain gets lodged in his throat. It's only a matter of seconds before he falls over the Playmate like a dead animal.

I approach him. I check his neck for a pulse.

"A heart attack or something," I conclude.

We push both bodies into the pit. We hear a distant sound approaching, approaching, approaching nearer and nearer.

•

Preceded by a noise of interference, the static returns and reaches us again. The great screen comes over us, passes through, and continues on its way, altering our contrast and brightness. On mute. I feel like running.

"I think you should go watch TV," El Autista suggests.

•

I run to the watchtower. *El Noticiero Nacional* hasn't ended, and there is no sign it ever will. El Coronel talks to the camera. El Coronel wears discreet but effective makeup: powder and eyelashes. His coiffed hair covers his shoulders, real breasts, and fake earrings. El Coronel is talking about an upcoming documentary, a superproduction: "a marvel of island engineering." I turn it up. With a perfect smile, El Coronel announces he's on the line with reporter Vida Guerra, who is now in . . .

I step back. I trip over a chair. I leave.

"Go ahead, Vida."

•

I see her. Holding a microphone, she approaches me. There are no cameras. Or maybe there are so many cameras I can no longer see them. I also can't tell where all the light is coming from. On the screen, to my left and suspended in the air near my arm, I see the logo of *El Noticiero* next to illuminated letters that spell "LIVE."

She walks, dragging her high heels, one crooked and the other missing. Her dress and arms are covered in lumps of dirt. Her eyes are two beads of opaque glass. She carries roaches and flies in her hair. Her body is covered with holes through which these insects go in and out.

Of course, I already know what she's going to ask me:

"Do you have anything to say regarding the construction of the Freeway?"

Vida Guerra brings the microphone to my face. I notice her bony hands. Her broken fingernails with chipped polish continue to grow. Her perfume becomes stronger.

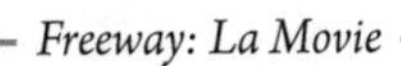

"No, nothing," I respond. But I could have just as easily said anything else. Breaking news. Nobody's going to understand what I'm trying to say, anyway.

El Hard Rock Live

But before the Freeway, nobody knows where from, the Seminole Indians had arrived.

I found them near the ruins of what once was La Tropical, over which a concert was being set up. The Farewell-to-Everything Concert. No more extreme metal, no more massive drunk brawls at the end of the night. A couple of emaciated guys I will never see again hammer the final nails into the rotted boards of the stage. I have a concert flyer in my hand: on one side, the musical lineup, and on the other, a bootleg vodka ad with a bottle smashed in half, blood dripping from its jagged edges.

ABSOLUT LA TROPICAL.

There are two Seminoles: an elderly one (you can see the entire tribe marching in protest in his wrinkles) and an expressionless younger one who I recognize immediately. It's El Autista in disguise. I ask myself what El Autista is doing with a Seminole Indian. Why is he pretending to be a Seminole Indian with a Seminole Indian who seems to be authentic?

At first (from far away), it looked like there were four Seminole Indians—but two were Subliminals, not Seminoles. You couldn't see their faces. There wasn't enough time. They explained their purpose was to appear in the documentary. They were just passing by, going back and forth, sending hidden messages to viewers in short segments.

•

Try Reggaetonic. Go to the corner bar, order a cold can of Reggaetonic soda, sit with old friends, with dear friends. Share the pain of your idle days, the pain of your hopeless days. Feel free to find comfort in the skyline of your pueblo, your city, your province. Wherever you are, there will always be a refreshing Reggaetonic waiting for you.

(Enjoy responsibly.)

•

"What are you doing?" I ask El Autista, who's looking at me solemnly.

"Good friend," El Seminole, the elderly one, addresses me. "We are looking for El Hard Rock Café." He unfurls before me, as if it were a flag, a faded red *Hard Rock Café Havana* T-shirt.

"From very far we come," El Autista intones. "We want find . . ."

"El Hard Rock Café no longer exists," I tell the Indian. "Your friend knows that very well. They demolished it. Look around. We're in the middle of an extreme makeover."

El Seminole turns his head, thoughtfully:

"Hmmm . . . I see. They're also filling the Florida Straits with rocks. Huge rocks, one over the next, over the cays. I suppose that is part of the Plan. What is hiding behind all this?"

"What could possibly be hiding?" I ask.

"The question is: Did the Cai-Men take this into account? We'll never know. El Hard Rock Café Havana was our last hope to understand."

"I can take you to the place where it once stood if you think contemplating its remains would be helpful."

"Good idea. You take us," El Autista says. "Perhaps there we find what we seek."

"You're coming with him, right?" I say with a fake smile, and he nods, and then El Seminole nods. There's nothing else to discuss. "Okay, let's go. We'll walk for many moons."

"The entire island?" The arthritic Seminole shudders.

"I'm kidding. We couldn't tour it even if we wanted to."

"Thank goodness, because we are exhausted. We have already traveled the entire world. Nearly the entire world—we have visited all of Los Hard Rock Cafés."

"What do the Seminoles have to do with El Hard Rock Café?" I ask, uninformed.

"You're joking, right? El Hard Rock Café International

has belonged to our tribe since the beginning of time. El Hard Rock Café is our tribe's home."

"And who are the Cai-Men? A specialist species of Seminole?"

"I suppose you could say that. They were the result of a genetic mutation in the Everglades."

"Their jaws were strong enough to crush the bones of small animals, but also so weak you could keep them from opening with your hand," El Autista Seminole reports to the camera following us.

"They're all dead now. We didn't get to know them well. The one who knew them best is also dead. He wasn't an Indian; he was a writer. His initials were P. K. D."

"The science fiction writer?" I ask.

Who else could it be? It couldn't be anybody else. Without a doubt, it has to be Philip Kindred Dick, the science fiction writer. Or simply Philip K.—"Science fiction writers, I am sorry to say, really do not know anything. We can't talk about science, because our knowledge of it is limited and unofficial, and usually our fiction is dreadful"—Dick, the Author.

•

In the mid-1970s, when he was still alive, he was eating at a Chinese restaurant in Yorba Linda, California, the town where Nixon grew up. In his fortune cookie, he got the following fortune:

DEEDS DONE IN SECRET HAVE A WAY OF BECOMING FOUND OUT.

He immediately mailed the slip of paper to the White House, mentioning that the Chinese restaurant was located within a mile of Nixon's original house.

I think a mistake has been made; by accident, I got Mr. Nixon's fortune. Does he have mine?

Signed: Philip K. Dick.

("That poor, poor man," he once said to his wife, Tessa, with tears in his eyes. "Shut up in the darkness, playing the piano in the night to himself, alone and afraid, knowing what's to come.")

The White House did not answer. The FBI had already stopped responding to his letters. He left the letters from the CIA unopened, for fear of miniature atomic bombs. The KGB kept invading his dreams with colorful lights.

The Cai-Men thought: *This guy is good.*

"Any little thing would trigger PKD's persecution complex," the Indian recalls. "That's why when the Cai-Men contacted him, he thought they were a secret organization planning to kidnap him."

The Cai-Men did, in fact, function as a secret organization within the Seminole tribe. And, due to Philip K. Dick's resistance to meet them, they did kidnap him. They took him away from Los Angeles—"I live near Disneyland," he once wrote. "They are always adding new rides and destroying old ones. Disneyland is an evolving organism."—to the swamps of the Everglades. When he saw the monstrous organisms that had captured him, the reptilian humanoids whose skin was covered with hard scales called osteoderms, he closed his eyes and said:

"A friend of mine once published a book called *Snakes of Hawaii*. A number of libraries wrote him, ordering copies. Well, there are no snakes in Hawaii. All the pages of his book are blank. I don't think you all exist; you're another one of my hallucinations. You're my blank pages."

The Cai-Men then placed a book in his hands. Philip K. Dick trembled. He sensed he had reached the pinnacle of his nightmare. But when he opened his eyes, he was surprised to see the book was a science fiction novel, one of his favorites—in his opinion, one of the greatest science fiction novels ever written.

The novel was *Camp Concentration* by Thomas Disch, also known as Tom—"I have a class theory of literature. I come from the wrong neighborhood to sell to *The New Yorker*. No matter how good I am as an artist, they always can smell where I come from" —Disch, Suicide Warrior.

•

Always keep a can of Reggaetonic in the fridge. After work, to combat the intense heat, take a cold shower and sit in front of the fan with a Reggaetonic soda in hand. Think of the cays brimming with hotels. Think of the hot mulatas and mulatos in swimsuits (their skin burning). Let the sweat hit the floor like drops of lead. Smile. Drink. Feel the dizziness dissipate, feel the tension of your neck melt away. Your head is not going to explode.

(Harmless if consumed in small sips.)

•

We walk. I end up being the tour guide of the disaster. The Subliminal Indians follow us at a distance. We arrive at the site marked HRC on the treasure map. The Seminoles search the rubble. In vain.

"This was it?" the elderly one asks, disappointed. "That's it?"

"The thing is, it was a compact restaurant," I tell him. I remember a bit, only a little bit, of what was inside:

Fender guitars hanging on the wall, some of them never used, some autographed, some autographed in extraterrestrial writing, or by a permanent marker with a life of its own. Rare photos of foreign bands, bands I was never able to identify, bands touring continuously through the provinces (in festivals sponsored, without anybody ever noticing, by a carbonated drink: the invisible drink you can only see in the background). A concert in the rain, in a vacant lot with trailers and cows. Five goths asleep in a dark park in Holguín. Four dinosaurs walking down a boulevard wearing dark glasses, letting the wind tousle their hair. A helicopter hovers over a crowd in a stadium. A guy who looks like Wilco's lead singer (or whose expression brings to mind the singer's migraines or the pharmaceutical addictions his migraines brought about) struggles with a crab in a Caibarién inn. A guy who looks like David Foster Wallace with a bandage across his head, in the middle of a burnt sugarcane field north of Ciego de Ávila. A gorgeous female guitarist hanging from a chain-link fence; in the background: La Bahía de Guantánamo, that remote place where the small town of Caimanera once stood.

Etcetera.

Lost photos and lost guitars. Memorabilia from when the Island seemed like a lunatic tour. From when the Island was, in the most profound way, a traumatic tour.

"What bad fortune is ours," El Autista Seminole declares. "Late we arrive. But arrive to where?"

They don't find anything, of course. Not under, over, or around the demolished restaurant.

"I still don't understand what you're looking for. A book?"

"It is possible that what we're looking for is in the form of a book with printed pages, although I doubt it." The elderly Seminole's eyes have grown even sadder. His wrinkles are now more pronounced. "It is possible that it is disguised as something hybrid or mutant since it was Cai-Men who decided to give it to Dick. We will never know." He takes a resigned pause and adds: "It's the content, not its form, that matters."

•

The secrets of the Cai-Men. Something only they knew. Something that could change the way we see the world. After the pause, we head out.

•

Rum and Reggaetonic. That's it. A party favorite. The mighty ally of popular dances. Indulge in debauchery. Vomit without shame. Vomit on yourself if necessary, but feel the quality and purity of the vomit. Go ahead, pass out—who cares? The next day you will not be alone; you'll be united forever with many drinkers in a nationwide hangover. That indestructible union is called Reggaetonic.

(If mixing with other beverages, do not exceed the recommended dose.)

•

"Conspiracy and cover-ups..." the Indian says, but the white man's words don't seem to satisfy him; they're descriptive but inadequate. "We hear about conspiracy theories and cover-ups all over the place. Nobody knows how, but the Cai-Men had accessed the Grand Unified Theory. The Theory from which all other theories might develop. The Theory in which all others might somehow be contained, like living cells. Yes, the Cai-Men had a primordial soup, a matrix, a flash point in their possession . . ."

It was shocking. Insane. Inconceivable. It had to do with the cash flow, with the shift of capital, with market economies. It had to do with a map—if it's possible to imagine something like a treasure map on which the treasure is moving all over the place or one on which, in the end, it isn't clear *what* the treasure actually is. Cash flow is, on this map, like a freeway. There are intersections, loops, detours. There is speed, abrupt declines, dimensional shifts. There is a sort of hidden pattern behind all of that, a pattern that jumps out like spots in two-dimensional gel electrophoresis—seemingly chaotic at first and then, all of a sudden: a shape appears when our focus shifts. And of course the junctions and nodes of that massive network are where the fetishes, the fixed ideas, all of our ravished bodies lurk. They're conducting all sorts of experiments on us that we'll never be able to imagine.

But what? Who? Why? For what?

Philip K. Dick felt farther and farther away from Disneyland (and Disneyland is everywhere). The Cai-Men told him: Take it step-by-step. Stay calm. And Philip K. Dick said: I feel as if I'm losing my mind. And they replied: There are many ways to lose one's mind. Haven't you noticed? And Philip K. Dick asked them if the truth was "out there," if the truth lies in the "desert of the real." And the Cai-Men told him they had had enough of his stupid questions; it was time to take action.

If taking action was possible.

"We believe the conspiracy between agent PKD and the Cai-Men" the Indian concludes in a serious voice, "consisted of waiting for a set date, a future event that would mark the beginning of a subversive and potentially liberating scheme in which he would play a central role. We believe this date took place at the beginning of this century. But agent PKD was already dead. He died a few years after meeting the Cai-Men."

Before dying, he attempted suicide twice. Before dying, he wrote several novels but never revealed anything about the conspiracy. He did reveal many other things. Too many.

Then the Cai-Men began to die. One by one, the mechanisms of their anomalous physiology began to fail. The last one of them revealed that the secret had been hidden in the last place anybody would look: the last Hard Rock Café.

El Hard Rock Café Havana.

•

El Autista breaks the silence:

"Cold blood."

"What?" I ask.

"The Cai-Men were cold-blooded beings."

I take out the concert flyer and show it to the Indian. He says:

"I cannot read. There is too much darkness for my eyes. What is it about?"

"It's the program for a rock concert tonight. I think we should go."

"Why?"

"It says there's going to be a band called the Caimen."

•

Tired? Fatigued? The new Reggaetonic soda is the answer. It contains vitamins, minerals, antidepressants; it's the latest fad in nutrition. Designed specially to boost your stamina. Don't let them seize your body or the bodies of others. Become an efferves-cent machine, a sexual steamroller. Try the new national drink: concentrated, energizing, hormonal . . .

(Avoid prolonged consumption.)

•

Spotlights come on as soon as we arrive. Nobody is on stage yet, but the cameras are aimed and ready.

A little girl suddenly appears. I guess she must be six or seven. Blond. She moves around consoles that appear to be too heavy for someone her size. She has extraordinary strength.

"Do you know them? Have you seen them before? Have you heard them?" the Indian asks me anxiously.

"Who?" I'm completely engrossed in watching the girl prodigy. She's like a mini model on an electronic runway.

"The Caimen . . . Are they a local band?"

"I have no idea. This is the first time I've heard of them."

A camera approaches us.

El Autista starts talking.

He talks to himself. He talks to the documentary.

He talks about searching until the end. He talks about the secrets of the Cai-Men, transformed into or scattered throughout innocent lyrics. He talks about the diabolical design in the circulation of money. He talks about the coded map, the key to a great continent. He talks about freeway flow dynamics that could explain virtually *everything*.

And he says everything as if he were an Indian.

Maybe he shouldn't talk about those things in that way (or in any other way). Just in case.

Meanwhile, the little girl has left the stage and joins us. But she's only interested in the real Indian. We can't fool her. She extends her hands to touch and stroke the old redskin's face. He calmly closes his eyes and allows the girl to slide the tips of her fingers over his wrinkles as if she were a blind person who could read something on his skin. The camera, perhaps unintentionally, captures the whole scene.

"Who are you?" El Seminole asks without opening his eyes.

"I'm the concert DJ," responds Little Miss DJ.

The concert is about to showcase (I shudder) the latest in Cuban rock.

I think:

Cuban rockers are the missing link of a chain that's more about food than about evolution.

Cuban rockers who once sang and recorded the one that goes like this: "*marchamos todos juntos / con la plaza llena / delante flota la bander / la lleva una niña con las tetas afuera . . .*"

Cuban rockers in a flashy video clip with a gigantic fembot that turns out to be none other than La Virgen de la Caridad del Cobre.

Cuban rockers build, brick by brick, a themed restaurant whose theme is themselves or the meticulous absence of a theme. A themed restaurant that is actually a front for an independent recording studio or a pirate radio station, which is itself a front for a real business: a lavish casino (linked to a prostitution ring) where Cuban rockers play all their chips—tiny chips, which are easy to hide, that look more like pebbles or colorful counting beads.

Cuban rockers on the other side of the most powerful telescopes.

Cuban rockers subjected to hypnosis, returning to school, reciting poetry every morning.

Cuban rockers trafficking files of unsolved cases from El Ministerio del Interior.

Cuban rockers confess: We are no longer rockers, we are no longer Cuban.

Cuban rockers ignited the memory of the Cuban rocker who climbed El Morro lighthouse, changed the light characteristics, and never came back down. He stayed there, alone, and watched all the ships sink.

Cuban rockers watching the latest weather forecast.

Cuban rockers charred by spontaneous combustion.

Cuban rockers as full of rage as they are empty of spite.

Cuban rockers strangled by their own (vocal) cords.

Cuban rockers in a catatonic state.

Cuban rockers who will never read this.

Cuban rockers no longer have nightmares.

•

A helicopter hovers over La Tropical and drops a ladder down.

Descending from the ladder, and then straight on the stage: Twiggy Ramírez.

Twiggy Ramírez looks old and skeletal. Definitely more Twiggy than Ramírez; he looks more like a wrecked model than a serial killer, more victim than assassin. He looks like he just stepped off an ancient planet where he took a beating. He looks as if he alone had swallowed the entire thrash-metal circuit of Florida and then purged it.

Twiggy slings on his Gibson guitar and grabs the microphone. The audience: the Seminole Indians, the Subliminal Indians, and myself. Five people, two of whom can't be perceived by the conscious mind. In any case, he shouts:

"Greetings to the Tribe!"

Followed by:

"Buenas noches, Havana!"

Followed by a profound silence from the audience.

"Well, bad news: The bands scheduled for tonight aren't going to play. Honestly, I don't know what happened to them. It must have been something awful. Although, if you think about it, this could be good news. Right?" Twiggy looks at the little girl and winks at her with his swollen eyelid and adds, "I'll be here for you to fill the gap, along with Niña DJ. We're going to improvise live, she and I, for you. Improvising, we're going to produce much more than just a concert: we're going to create a desert. Isn't that right, Niña DJ? Let's do this, La Tropicaaaaaal!!!"

•

I try to comfort El Seminole. In any case, I tell him, we would've had to sit through a dozen awful bands before getting to the Caimen. The old man keeps his eyes closed; I'm not sure if he's listening to me, but he nods anyway. He doesn't need words. It's almost as if he's listening to something else, a sound on a different scale. It's almost as if he's ready to die right now, at this very moment. And die happy.

•

I am Reggaetonic. Before the Freeway existed, I existed. I am the Word, and my name shall not be uttered. It is a name unknown to all. They call me Reggaetonic, but Reggaetonic is not my name. I am. I will always be.

El Transmetal

The Freeway needs builders. The locals need money.

El Autista goes into the employment office. A robust woman, carved out of marble with a chisel and hammer, greets him.

El Autista comes out a bit later, shaking:

"They've let me go."

They never even hired him. The woman gave him an IQ test and then a psychometric personality test. She told him he wasn't fit for the job.

"The job only requires moving things from one place to another," El Autista argued.

Signing a little piece of paper, the woman told El Autista that she was referring him to a place where they could help him. They had *specialists*. She told him High Command had established clear guidelines for determining who could build the Great Freeway and who couldn't.

"High Command," repeated El Autista, with his peculiar way of repeating words that immediately confirms his diagnosis, whatever it may be. For her part, the woman couldn't tell him who was in the High Command, or from where they commanded, or what the guidelines were.

Now I go into the office. The woman looks at me and asks me not to waste her time. She can't offer me a job.

"Why not?"

"You very well know why. Next!"

•

We can't work in construction, but we can look at Los Transformer robots. Los Constructicons, they're called. They're enormous. They walk across the ravaged land like beasts of war. They're the heavyweights of the nonfiction engineering film. They look like toys from a distance. They lift and move structures, and every so often, they gracefully transform into bulldozers, excavators, dump trucks, cement mixers, steamrollers, cranes, etcetera.

•

The workers are careful not to get trampled by Los Transformers. Attracted by this work of historic proportions, they don't just come from the North but from all the surrounding areas. They swarm in: Mexicans, Central Americans, Dominicans, Haitians, Puerto Ricans, natives of the Bahamas, from Grand Cayman, from Jamaica, from the Islands and coasts trampled by the fury of hurricanes.

•

A guy with a Mexican accent approaches me:

"What team are you on, compañero?"

"I'm not working."

"They didn't cast you?"

"What casting?"

"Those sons of a chingada madre don't even show their faces."

"They sent my friend straight to the psych ward," I add to his complaint. "They've probably confined him to a cell by now."

"They do have good medical facilities, that's for sure. Great camps where they have everything. Any drug you want. What do you need? I can't help you, but I know some guys."

"I'm not looking to buy anything. I don't have any money."

"Oh, so do you want to make some cash? I need another assistant."

El Mexicano, Hu Jintao, had come to the Island with a beardless fifty-something who responded to the name "Poppy." Hu Jintao was an engineer who belonged to Los Tecnócratas, the ones known for controlling and repairing Los Transformers. Poppy assisted him with as much dedication as ineffectiveness. He didn't understand machines. He didn't understand Los Transformers.

"But Poppy cooks very well, and I care about him," Hu Jintao tells me. "A bit after we met, he confessed he had fallen in love with me. I made it clear I was 100 percent heterosexual but that we could be friends. Since then, he has been a faithful companion. The thing is . . . he makes me nervous. I don't know anything about his past except that he's from the United States. I don't think Poppy is his real name. I think he's a fugitive."

A rumor that *something* is approaching circulates in English and in Spanish among the workers. The radars have picked it up. Nobody knows for sure what the radars are, or where they are, or even what it is they've seen. But it's approaching.

And one fine day it appears on the horizon, to the west, under the clouds, in the Gulf.

It is a gigantic woman, colossal . . .

It is a woman of tropospheric proportions.

"She's a robot," some shout.

"She's a blow-up doll," others shout.

"She's a hurricane," Hu Jintao says, and they all stare at him, agape. El Mexicano turns to me, his face deformed with terror, and adds: "This is what I was trying to warn you about. This is what the Island Machine makes."

•

At Universidad Tecnológica de Cancún, Hu Jintao had been the student of a brilliant scientist. More than brilliant: a scientific genius. Hu Jintao referred to him simply as "El Profesor." A feeble old man with a white beard and an aura of local celebrity that followed him everywhere. Hu Jintao professed absolute admiration.

One day, El Profesor asked him to join a secret project. Hu Jintao accepted immediately, of course, and went to Isla Mujeres with El Profesor. Once there, he found himself in an enormous lab equipped with the most advanced technology. Technology he had never even dreamed of.

"Híjole, I had no idea there could be a lab like this in México," he said when he recovered his words and accent. "Or in any other part of the world."

"Very few know about it," El Profesor said. "From now on, keep it a secret, or it'll cost you your life."

"Profesor, are you in charge of all this?"

"Yes, you can say I'm in charge. And I am the guardian angel. I am the mastermind. I am the origin. I am the creator of all this. Do you know how long I've been working here?"

"Working on what, Profesor?" Hu Jintao was getting nervous.

"This way. I'll show you something you'll like . . . or not."

They descended to the subterranean levels. Hallways. Control rooms with long panels. Operators in white lab coats. Very few, given the magnitude of the place. Most were Chinese. They finally reached a type of microwave oven whose size was beyond all comparison. The schematics showed that it was connected to a funnel, kilometers long—much like a particle accelerator—that would end up in the Caribbean Sea, in the Yucatán Channel.

"Here is where we collect hurricanes, and then we transform them," El Profesor said.

The process involved reconnaissance planes that would "capture" the hurricane, the hurricane essence, with a thorough scan of its structure and variables. All of which was then cloned in the microwave.

"What are they transformed into?"

"It depends on the name. Those with female names are transformed into women, rather exaggerated women. What else can you expect from a woman with hurricane DNA? Those with male names, however, we have never been able to transform into men or into anything else. It just doesn't work the same way. I do not know why this happens. This is where you come in. Your job will be to figure out the problem, to help me fix this small glitch."

But Hu Jintao found something else on that island. Love. From the moment he laid eyes on El Profesor's daughter, he couldn't think about the masculine transformation problem anymore.

Or even about the masculine gender in general.

El Profesor introduced her as his daughter, but Hu Jintao doubted she was. She was young enough to be his granddaughter, and, also, they didn't look anything alike. El Profesor looked like a former Nazi official with very pale skin and little blue eyes, magnified by the thick lenses of his glasses. She, on the other hand, was a voluptuous Indian woman with big black eyes and large breasts; she was an authentic beauty, uncolonized. Hu Jintao thought of Ixchel, the Mayan goddess. Almost as if he could read Hu Jintao's thoughts, El Profesor told him his daughter was, in fact, the goddess Ixchel, but that he affectionately called her Chely.

As one might expect, Hu Jintao and Chely became lovers. They kept it from El Profesor. Hu Jintao didn't think they should sneak around, but Chely said it would be best if her father didn't find out so soon. She asked him to trust her, so he agreed to keep the relationship a secret, thinking the secret would soon become public.

It didn't take long for El Profesor to find them naked in bed together.

"Traitor! That's how you repay me? And after all I've done for you? Stealing my daughter's virginity!"

Hu Jintao, dumbfounded, was sure this had to do with a hidden camera prank. What else could it be? But El Profesor was now charging at him with a knife, and so, he chose to run out of the room.

El Profesor ran after him. Since arriving at the island, Hu Jintao had noticed certain changes in the scientist's personality. It was almost as if the cliché of the mad, evil scientist who wants to take over the world had begun to seep out of his pores. He now realized the psychopath in El Profesor had completely awoken.

And he was a tireless psychopath at that. Hu Jintao, with El Profesor after him, ran through the entire maze of absurd installations until he succumbed to exhaustion. Finally, he was able to hide in a storage area and there, luckily, Chely found him first.

"You have to leave, mi amor. I drew you a map so you would know how to get to the yacht anchored on the other end of the island. Board quickly and get as far away from here as you can."

Hu Jintao understood it was too late to act sensibly.

"Chely, you didn't tell me you were a virgin."

"Because I've never been a virgin. Which means I've always been a virgin, more or less. According to the Catholics, anyway, I've been one for centuries. Do you understand? You know, the Blessed Virgin and all of that. But none of that matters now. If you don't leave, my father will keep looking for you, and when he finds you, he'll kill you."

The yacht set sail from Isla Mujeres, but it didn't get far. As soon as the fugitive discovered (over by Cayo Largo, at the entrance of the Gulf of Batabanó) the pillars of what would be a great freeway over the sea, he completely forgot about his escape. He had found the titanic project that matched his skills.

Hu Jintao volunteers to confront the hurricane. If someone has to do it, he tells Los Tecnócratas and the workers gathered there, it has to be him. It is Hu Jintao the hurricane has come for. The hurricane is there to kill him. He is going to fight for his life, and he is going to fight for the future, so not even a meter of the construction will be delayed. We have to stop the hurricane from destroying everything. (Everything has already been destroyed.)

•

It starts to drizzle. The wind picks up.

I take shelter with Poppy in the back of a shipping container.

I thought El Mexicano was terrified, but Poppy is even more terrified.

"Nothing is going to happen that hasn't happened before," I tell him. "And when it's over, even if you don't believe it, we'll still be here."

In the battlefield, a subgroup of transformers called Los Combiners has transformed their bodies to join and create El Súper Robot Transformer, which is much bigger, stronger, and more powerful. And up there, inside his head and behind his eyes, is the cabin from where El Mexicano controls the robot's movements.

Approaching El Súper Robot is the extraordinary Hussicane: dressed in a ripped babydoll, frayed, tattered, with a low neckline that barely covers her enormous breasts and two shiny pink boots that shake the earth with every step. She wears heavy makeup, and her hair, long, blonde, loose . . .

"That's quite a look," I comment.

Poppy is on the verge of a nervous breakdown.

Still, he says:

"It's kinderwhore. A joke of a joke."

"What?" This is the first time I hear him speak. He has a very delicate voice.

"A kindergarten prostitute. A little-girl puta. The image of US female punk rock bands of the last decade of the twentieth century. Courtney Love was the one who started the trend."

I begin to better understand Poppy's fears.

"She . . . the Hussicane . . . Is it Courtney Love?"

"No. She's Katrina."

•

In antediluvian times, Poppy was happy in New Orleans. He had a career as a successful writer and lived in a beautiful house in the French Quarter with his partner, a chef who also had a successful career (Poppy referred to him as "his husband"). Then Katrina hit, and Poppy moved to a safe place on the other side of the Mississippi. A few weeks later, he returned to New Orleans and restored his beautiful house, and it seemed as if everything would go back to normal.

But it didn't.

Nothing would ever be the same again.

The dead were now there.

The dead from Katrina began to appear in Poppy's dreams. They wouldn't let him sleep. Poppy would then get out of bed and turn on the TV to listen to preachers. One, Fred Phelps, founder of Westboro Baptist Church, claimed Katrina had been

God's wrath against the sins of the South, against the United Sins of America, and especially against the homosexuals:

"New Orleans, symbol of America, seen for what it is: a putrid, toxic, stinking cesspool of fag fecal matter. Pray for more dead bodies floating on the fag-semen-rancid waters of New Orleans."

The dead appeared to Poppy. To a Poppy who was ever more awake. In the bathtub, on the furniture, under the beds, behind the curtains, inside the freezer in his husband's restaurant.

Some of the dead were very decomposed—they had a putrid stench and were inexpressive. Other dead bodies were your typical living dead. Zombies of the swamp covered in mud.

And the zombies would tell him: Write now.

And the zombies would tell him: Have you seen the horror? The horror? Watch and learn.

The time is now. Now you know what you have to write. Now you'll understand what it means to write.

Poppy knew it, that's true, but he couldn't bring himself to do it. He wasn't able to write a single word. He let his readers down: the alternative chicks who read his books in Southern universities, the gothic kids, the Marilyn Manson fans. These fans came together immediately after the hurricane—when there was still no news—to raise funds, to send him provisions, and to look for his body in the morgues. He failed the dead, he failed all the floating bodies waiting for stories that would clear the pipes, the dead who would never (he knew it, now out of breath, shaking, sweating, collapsing) stop harassing him to *write*. So, he fled.

But he had to radically flee.

Step one: Leave New Orleans, leave the country.

Step two: Get a new identity, get a sex change.

"Oh, yeah, I was born female," Poppy tells me. "But even though I lived for many years as a biological woman, I've always completely felt like a man. I just never tried to dress as such or to look like a man on the outside. What for? Until I had no other choice . . ."

Somewhere in Texas, before crossing the border and penetrating into México, Poppy Z. Brite, whose real name is Melissa Ann Brite (former writer of bestsellers, former champion of women's rights, former model, and former stripper, who wrote on her blog when she was still a woman that she was comfortable with the term "nonoperative transsexual"), got on a testosterone diet, had gender reassignment surgery, and brought out the man within: the man he had always been.

And now, Poppy ran with him.

•

In the last decade of the twentieth century, Poppy Z. Brite, the female version, reached a sort of notoriety in the genre of horror.

Lost Souls, the first novel, was about vampires. Neo-Gothic and hypersexualized, with some innovations to Anne Rice's model: older vampires have naturally sharp teeth, as it should be, are sensitive to sunlight, and can't eat or drink. On the other hand, young vampires have regular human teeth that must be filed, are not sensitive to sunlight, and can eat and drink whatever they want. Nothing is a teenage vampire raised by humans, on a journey to find his real family. Nothing's father (and also his lover) is Zillah, an androgynous vampire described as an incredibly beautiful creature with black nails and nipple piercings.

Drawing Blood is about a comic book artist, a bisexual hacker, and a lost community in North Carolina. Urban legend has it that a fire in a Los Angeles mail store permeated several copies of this novel with the smell of burnt flesh. A dealer then sold them as collectibles.

Exquisite Corpse contains cannibalism, necrophilia, voodoo, and lewd, shallow boys. But it's a love story. The protagonist is a gay serial killer (based on the psychopath Dennis Nilsen) who finds his soulmate (based on the psychopath Jeffrey Dahmer) in the French Quarter. According to the book's back cover, this story "leaves a trail of blood from London to the USA."

The Lazarus Heart is based on the universe and themes of *The Crow,* the comic book series created by James O'Barr, a metal rocker from Detroit. He created it as a way to cope with the death of his fiancée, who was run over by a drunk driver.

The Crow, a product of O'Barr's depression, becomes the icon for contemporary gothic culture. A homosexual named Jared is wrongly executed for the murder of his lover. He is then resurrected by The Crow to avenge and bring justice to the real killer. His lover's twin brother, a transwoman (so, actually, his lover's twin sister), helps Jared on his mission. Then the movie came out: *The Crow: Salvation*. This was Kirsten Dunst's (the transgender twin) debut in a comic book movie before she ever appeared in the *Spider-Man* trilogy.

Plastic Jesus changes the tune a little bit. The plot takes place in the sixties. Seth and Peyton, singers of the rock quartet the Kydds, fall madly in love with each other and make their relationship public after the Stonewall Riots, compromising the band's popularity. Of course, it was all really a way of having a parallel discussion about the Beatles and the hypothetical intimate relationship between John and Paul. Of course, one must always discuss certain things in parallel.

•

"All this because of the change," someone says.

"What change?" someone else asks.

"Climate change. Local warming."

The match starts to heat up. Katrina and Transformer Hu Jintao jump around from side to side in a whirlwind of punches. Katrina is covered in scrapes and bruises from the metal-on-metal impact, but that's about it. An impartial spectator would bet on her, no doubt. Even if only because her beastly kicks, which rattle her opponent's head, allow us to catch—high in the sky and under the white cloud by her thighs—a quick glimpse of her little-girl bloomers.

"There must be a Japanese word for visions like these . . ."

"They're not visiones, güey. They're presiones."

•

Later on, Poppy Z. Brite transitions to a new genre: black comedy. This time, Poppy writes novels like *Liquor*, *Prime*, and *Soul Kitchen*, all set in the gastronomic universe of New Orleans. The protagonists are two gay cooks who are addicted to tequila.

•

We're now an official disaster area. What we always have been. The air we breathe in the containers is now saturated with the scent of violence . . .

"The United States government controls hurricanes. With airplanes and probes and such things. They program their intensity and course trajectory."

"If Hu Jintao is inside El Transformer's head, who's inside the Blonde's?"

"Blondes, despite their size, have nothing inside their heads."

"Who controls them?"

"Remote controls . . ."

"What matters is their mission, not who's controlling them."

"This is all an effort to delay the Great Freeway, you can be sure."

"Didn't you understand anything I said? The US government?"

"Under these circumstances, nothing is well understood. Something in the air."

•

Outside of pop fiction (though not too far), Poppy Z. Brite wrote articles, essays, recipes, including *Courtney Love: The Real Story*, a biography of Kurt Cobain's widow. But just as any story is never the *real* story, one could suppose Courtney Love would have hated it with all of her being. Years later, the widow published *Dirty Blonde: The Diaries of Courtney Love*, a memoir that includes poetry, song lyrics, notes, photographs, clippings, collages, letters, emails, etcetera.

I found my inner bitch and ran with her.

I like there to be some testosterone in rock, and it's like I'm the one in the dress who has to provide it.

I am not a woman. I'm a force of nature.

All around Katrina and Hu Jintao, circling like projectiles: pieces of boards, zinc sheets, plastic tanks, hard hats and tools, bricks, ropes, cables, old sacks, grocery bags from a supermarket from the other end of the world, piles of garbage, and every now and then, a humble Antillean worker, shipwrecked and naked with a broken spine.

"He used to say that Indian woman was a goddess," Poppy tells me. "But the closest thing to a goddess he'll ever see in his life is that thing in front of him that's going to kill him."

A dirty goddess in a dirty fight. Katrina has invincible strength and agility. El Transformer, with his damaged mechanisms, gets up from the muck again and again. El Transformer launches missiles, shoots rays, attempts to shield himself with useless forcefields . . .

"We haven't lost him yet," I tell Poppy. But he knows that's not true. It's time for the final count.

He met Hu Jintao in the Riviera Maya (traveling all over México, faithfully following the North American tradition of heading south). They became fast friends. They drank tequila. They shared an apartment. Poppy decided to settle in for a while, look for a job in a hotel, take advantage of any opportunity for love. Hu Jintao easily tolerated his homosexuality, but he couldn't tolerate all the books he read to learn Spanish: his old colleagues' novels in translation. Hu Jintao would tell him they were all commercial shit, nothing but bus- and gas-station novels.

"Then he would pick up Kafka," Poppy recalls, "and read passages to me from 'The Great Wall of China.' His favorite."

•

In those days many people, and among them the best, had a secret maxim which ran: Try with all your might to comprehend the decrees of the high command, but only up to a certain point; then avoid further meditation.

In the office of the command—where it was and who sat there no one whom I have asked knew then or knows now—in that office one may be certain that all human thoughts and desires revolved in a circle, and all human aims and fulfillments in a countercircle.

Far rather do I believe that the high command has existed from all eternity, and the decision to build the wall likewise. Unwitting peoples of the north, who imagined they were the cause of it! Honest, unwitting Emperor, who imagined he decreed it! We builders of the wall know that it was not so and hold our tongues.

"He was naive and charming," Poppy added. "Like a boy."

Katrina beats him mercilessly and enjoys it. Like a girl.

Katrina scratches him, causes the metal to spark, cracks him open . . .

Katrina moves so fast she becomes invisible.

"Then came the job on the mysterious island." Poppy

went to Isla Mujeres with Hu Jintao. There was nothing to do in the cabin near the laboratory except wait and be bored. Hu Jintao would leave for work in the morning. And after work, he wouldn't stop talking about the divine Indian woman, the one of pornographic proportions. And one afternoon, the Indian woman appeared at the cabin, the Blessed Miss México in the flesh (who was, of course, as ordinary as any other Latina). She told Poppy that Hu Jintao would meet him at a yacht anchored on the coast. Poppy waited for two days that seemed more like two months before he saw Hu Jintao running toward him. Naked.

They set sail.

This disaster concludes their journey.

Now, when it's too late, a couple of military planes come to El Transformer's aid. It's not clear what they're going to do. Confuse her? Cool her down? Katrina unleashes her Category 5 swipes and makes them crash.

"But there is something he doesn't know," Poppy tells me.

"I'm sure there are a bunch of things none of us know, things we will never know," I tell him with a heavy heart as I watch the planes.

"This isn't the Indian woman's fault. This is all my fault."

Brite describes sumptuous meals at swanky restaurants and icy death with equal aplomb, and her stories are spirited and snappy. (Booklist)

Among Poppy Z.'s books, it's important to mention

Wrong Things, a collection of stories co-written with Caitlín Kiernan, a translesbian from Providence, Rhode Island—Lovecraft's homeland.

Kiernan has a vast range of interests. She is the former vocalist and lyricist of a Georgia-based Southern goth-folk-blues band, Death's Little Sister (whose name is based on Neil Gaiman's character). Her writing spans a wide range of genres, from science fiction to so-called dark fantasy, to DC Comics, to paleontology. She was the first to describe the *Selmasaurus russelli*, a new species of mosasaur (*mosasaur* means "terrifying monster"). In the article, "Stratigraphic Distributions and Habitat Segregation of Mosasaurus in the Upper Cretaceous of Western and Central Alabama, with an Historical Review of Alabama Discoveries," published in *Journal of Vertebrate Paleontology*, she writes about the mosasaurs of the Deep South.

Mosasaurs were huge carnivorous reptiles that lived in all of the world's oceans during the Late Cretaceous period.

Caitlín Kiernan once wrote on her blog:

"I'm getting tired of telling people that I'm not a 'horror' writer."

•

What the cameras see now:

A desolate landscape. A gigantic fallen robot. Katrina standing over his remains, with hair completely disheveled, in a tattered babydoll that doesn't cover her enormous, battered, naked body, her flesh covered with smoking holes and fibers. She looks into the void. She gazes at the horizon over her shoulder. The clouds dissipate.

A figure approaches her. It's Poppy.

Poppy reaches Katrina's feet.

Poppy looks up to the sky and whispers:

"Here I am, bitch. Look. It's me."

•

Marilyn Manson, for the documentary:

"New Orleans is the cesspool of America. If you avoid the tourist attractions, you will only find unsightliness: perverse and disfigured people, freaks, drug addicts, repugnant transsexuals . . . I've never seen a town with so many trashy vampires, desperate folks who believe they're Anne Rice characters or some other writer's."

MM pauses.

MM looks at the camera again and adds:

"You've got to be desperate. Right?"

La White Trash

•

And the construction continues relentlessly. As the Freeway takes shape, it displaces tons of debris into its banks. Mountains of debris, scattered by the constant roar of construction, extending for kilometers and kilometers. One of those formations, the greatest one, they call El Vertedero. Intelligent life can be found there: Some are passing through (exploration, boredom, fatigue), others are permanent residents. I run into a couple of almost identical Black men exhaling smoke out of their noses. Rastas. They erected a shelter out of cardboard and zinc sheets. One wears a large crocheted cap, and the other has live snakes growing out of his head. The one in the cap greets me. I ask him if we know each other.

"We've been here for several days, hermano," he reports.

•

El Autista has been in El Vertedero for several days. Before that, he was in a sort of medical facility, he tells me: "in the entrails of a monstrous polyclinic," where nobody knew what to do with him until they finally discharged him. But he continues (and will continue) to be treated.

"What happened while I was gone?" he asks.

"A strong hurricane hit. I'm not sure La Habana could have resisted it."

"Listen," he says as he gestures with his arms so dramatically that it looks like he's trying to pick up the breeze that comes from the desert, from beyond the dump sites, and scatter it like dust from the other side, over the foundation of the Freeway that can be seen in the distance. "Listen to the silence beneath the noise of the machines. It's the sound of La Habana resisting."

I immediately ask:

"What's the diagnosis? What kind of insanity do you suffer from?"

"I have this," El Autista shows me a medium-sized hardcover notebook. "I have to write down my innermost thoughts. For therapy. So, I designed a line of notebooks." A round seal embossed on its cover: DB. "You hold in your hand a genuine Dirty Blonde Notebook. Leaf through it and feel the consistency, the weight. I have a bunch of them."

"You're going to revolutionize the market," I tell him.

I'm not sure which market I'm referring to.

•

The other part of the treatment takes place face-to-face with a Therapist.

Therapist 2.0: a popular virtual therapy program, a holographic projection that interacts with the patient. It's the latest.

El Autista presses a button, and then she appears, in all her glorious dimensions: from top to bottom, seated on a couch, legs crossed and hair coiffed, a woman in her forties with fancy glasses and an intellectual presence.

You can see through her, but you don't want to see through her.

"All this psychology and everything else is crap," a voice says behind us.

Almost identical, almost indistinguishable, except one wears that large crocheted cap. We don't know which Rasta just spoke.

"We're not Rastas," the one not wearing the cap says, startled. The black snakes are agitated, moving every which way, looking in every direction.

"Which one of you is the patient?" La Therapist asks.

El Autista points at me.

•

La Therapist: Good. How have you been?

El Autista:

La Therapist: We can start by talking about what you've written . . .

El Autista:

La Therapist: In your notebook. Do you have a notebook already?

El Autista: Not one, many. I have a whole line of notebooks.

La Therapist: Excellent. The important thing now is to take one of those notebooks and start writing . . .

El Autista: I don't know if I can. It'll never just be a notebook for me. Everything I write will attract versions and variations that could be written simultaneously in thousands of other notebooks that carry my seal. It's too much, even for the greatest.

La Therapist:

El Autista:

La Therapist: Writing your thoughts down will give you perspective. It will help you to understand your feelings, to analyze them. That's the idea. Don't you think it might be helpful? Aren't you interested in analyzing yourself?

El Autista:

La Therapist:

El Autista: I would be more interested in analyzing the Rastas.

•

Another key in distinguishing them is in the way each one handles weed. The one in the crocheted cap makes his joint by rolling the weed into the paper, smoking it, exhaling spirals of colors: red, purple, violet smoke, smoke that changes tones and smells sweet. The other one dices the weed into little bits and puts the pieces into the mouths of the snakes on his head. He says the snakes are strict vegetarians. I suppose the chewed-up weed is digested and, from there, first goes through his head, and then into his brain. I'm not sure which of the two is the parasite.

The most interesting thing, however, is the colorful smoke from the weed. The Rastas tell us it's highly radioactive. It grows in El Vertedero.

We go to take a look:

Among the junk and waste, with fluorescent leaves and stems . . .

"What is this?" asks El Autista.

Next to the plant, poking through the sand, there is a buried bone.

We dig.

"It looks like a femur," I say.

"You can find anything here," brags one of the Rastas.

"Maybe there's more," says El Autista.

We move sand, rocks, debris, and we find long bones and short bones, clavicles, kneecaps, metacarpus, vertebrae, hip transplants, plates, and little bits of crania. Little by little, we unearth and dust off a complete skeleton.

•

El Autista: Do you know anything about paleontology?

La Therapist: It is not my area of expertise.

El Autista: Are you an expert in anything?

La Therapist:

El Autista:

La Therapist: Are you interested in . . . fossils?

El Autista: We found the remains of a humanoid under El Vertedero. I think it's an extinct species.

La Therapist: On the American continent, no human remains date back more than fifteen thousand years. Tell me about the place where you found it. El Vertedero?

El Autista: Certainly, something like cancer must have brought them to extinction. A slow and painful death. Death by overexposure.

La Therapist:

El Autista:

La Therapist:

El Autista:

La Therapist: Then . . . is this species related to Neanderthals, or to *Homo sapiens*?

El Autista: I've named him *Homo cubensis*.

•

The Rastas assure us they had nothing to do with the skeleton. They haven't killed or buried anybody. They're poor musicians, poor poets, poor painters, starving locals of this area, from right here, from La Habana del Este. They don't know anything, and nobody has ever offered them a peso to keep their mouths shut. They cough. They cough. (A cloud of colors casts a shadow over the shelter's surroundings.)

•

El Autista [tapping on the cover of the DB notebook]: I have been taking notes, making observations . . .

La Therapist: Excellent. Would you like to share them?

El Autista: The characteristics that distinguish *Homo cubensis* from its closest primate relatives (the gorilla, the chimpanzee, the orangutan, and the *Homo sapiens*) are due to a very early adaptation of an erect posture and a manner of walking that only uses the hind extremities (bipedalism). The spinal column places the center of gravity just above the supporting surface of the feet, which provides stability. How much stability? That, I can't precisely say. Doctor, I can imagine what you must be thinking: Why this obsession with stability? Isn't it enough that the *Homo cubensis* could stand on its two feet and walk?

La Therapist:

El Autista: Bipedalism frees up the hands, which then become very sensitive tools, capable of manipulating objects with great precision. A pen for writing, a spray can for graffiti, a blade for cutting flesh. The most important structural detail is the thumb, which is elongated, opposable, and has a wide range of motion.

La Therapist:

El Autista:

La Therapist [moving her transparent thumbs]: So, when you said "observations" you were referring to . . .

El Autista: To the species I discovered? Yes.

La Therapist: Have you considered the possibility that this species of yours may not really exist? That it's a figment of your imagination?

El Autista:

La Therapist:

El Autista [pensively]: The brain . . .

La Therapist: That's what I'm referring to. Your mind, and all the things that have grown in it. Weeds we have to pull. We can do it together.

El Autista: Based on the cranium, the brain of the *Homo cubensis* would have been large (an average volume of fourteen hundred cc). More or less twice the size of its ancestors. This presents all sorts of complications. The need to consume many more calories, for example. There has always been a shortage of calories in its environment. A large cranium also requires anatomical modifications for the offspring to go through the birth canal. Thus, the *Homo cubensis* female pelvis would have had to notably expand at maturity, which would have resulted in peculiar locomotion, particularly on high heels.

La Therapist: I see. The specimen of this species you found, is it female?

El Autista: No.

La Therapist: Young?

El Autista: Quite the contrary. The bones are very worn.

•

The Rastas examine their DB notebooks, one for each of them, and then ask El Autista:

"How much?"

"I'm not selling them to you. It's a gift. So you'll use them. So you can write down your thoughts."

"Thank you, hermano. You noticed we're intellectuals."

"You'll let me know if the notebooks are any good. I want you to give me honest Rasta feedback."

They hold back and look at him long and hard:

"Don't say that."

"We're not Rastas."

The silence expands, it thickens . . .

"But you're thinking about selling them—a business, right?"

"I . . . I could try to do that," El Autista stutters.

"Open a stationery shop with the latest notebooks. Or even better: a bookstore. And finally . . . to have . . . to have some money . . ." the one with the brood of snakes on his head sighs through their mouths. "I mean, how can you compare ripping off a book to opening a bookstore?"

"Or to writing a book—writing a book that turns out to be worse than theft," the other adds. "Writing a book that appears to hold the original book that you meant to rip off responsible."

"I'm going to start taking notes on a story I've always wanted to write. A secret story. Do you know what it's about?"

El Autista and I say we don't at the same time, imagining things that scare us.

"The history of homemade technology in my country," the Rasta announces.

•

El Autista: The physical adaptations allowed the *Homo cubensis* to be more active than other primates. They also facilitated the development of a wide range of abilities and versatile behavior incomparable to the rest of the world. The large brain size gave way to the stereotypical and instinctive behavior that can be modified by training. The changes in the middle were the result of quick adjustments and not of genetic selection. This is how survival was possible in extreme conditions and in a wide range of habitats, without the need for additional differentiation of the species. That is resistance. That's where la cultura comes in, understood as the capacity to transmit information between generations by exogenous means. It is important to note that la cultura developed notably for the *Homo cubensis*. Until, of course, la cultura reached its end.

La Therapist: I see you went beyond the skeleton.

El Autista: That was the idea.

La Therapist: The interest you have for this species is impressive, and the language you use to describe it. What do you think that means?

El Autista:

La Therapist:

El Autista: Have you listened to a single word I've said?

•

I discuss the notebooks with El Autista. DB isn't a registered trademark (it's only two capital letters), but he should expect corporate conflict. Dirty Blonde Notebooks should protect its identity against Dumb Blonde Notebooks, for example.

El Autista doesn't seem worried. He has anticipated the confusion. Dirty Blonde will always be in conflict with Dumb Blonde, and it is precisely this conflict that will define each style.

Assuming the two DB notebooks are the same color, have the same dimensions, are molecularly identical, one would have to read its contents to determine which one is the Dumb Blonde, and which one is the Dirty Blonde. And one would have to read with the eyes of an expert, or better yet, with the eyes of an addict, to notice the differences.

•

El Autista: My hypothesis is that *Homo cubensis* lived almost its entire existence in the Stone Age.

La Therapist:

El Autista: Throughout the Paleolithic, the *Homo cubensis* would have been a poor hunter and gatherer. Probably also fished.

La Therapist: What did they hunt?

El Autista: Herbivores.

La Therapist: That's it?

El Autista:

La Therapist:

El Autista: I see. It's a trick question.

•

There isn't much to do here.

The Rastas smoke. They walk their extremely thin shadows from one end to the other. They play with their beaded necklaces.

El Autista plays with the skeleton as if it were a model meant to build and take apart.

The Rastas ask him:

"Do you know who the dead body is?"

"Do you know?"

"No."

"Why would I know?"

"It was only a question."

"I have no way of answering that. The evidence is taking me in a different direction."

"And you're following the evidence. And you don't know who the dead body is."

"Yes. No."

"Hey, about that psychiatrist of yours . . ."

"She's virtual."

"But she's foreign, right?"

"She's virtual."

"Yuma?"

•

There isn't much to do here.

Dig?

Writing, obviously, is impossible.

I don't know what El Autista is writing in his DB notebook. When I asked him about therapy and if he was writing down the thoughts coming to him, he told me it had been a long time (millions of years) since he last had any thoughts of his own. He let me read his notes, and now I have his DB notebook. I don't dare open it.

•

The Rastas now have a word for El Autista: antropoloco.

—La Therapist [looking around with a devastated look on her face]: Is this where you live? In this shack?

El Autista: Groups of *Homo cubensis* of the Paleolithic must have been extremely nomadic. They lived safely in small encampments, caves, rock shelters, rudimentary shelters. Although I would be surprised to find evidence of tents and cabins from the Upper Paleolithic Period. But then there would also have to be evidence of complex burial practices. This is not the case of the specimen we exhumed unless El Vertedero itself is massive burial evidence . . . Yes, that must be it.

La Therapist: You repeated the word "evidence" three times.

El Autista: Oh. I wonder what the repetition means.

La Therapist:

El Autista: On the other hand, I estimate the *Homo cubensis* started using fire around 1.5 million years ago. At first, as a source of light and heat, to cook food and protect themselves from wild animals. As time went on, they would use it to alter the color of mineral pigments, bake clay figures (and later to sell paintings and crafts to foreigners), and commit suicide. I sense the females of this species were prone to burning themselves.

La Therapist: But is the specimen you found female or not?

El Autista: Have you treated suicide survivors?

La Therapist: Basta ya, okay? You know exactly what you're doing.

El Autista:

La Therapist: You're getting off track. You're telling me a whole imaginary story to evade your own story. The real story.

•

El Autista wrote in his notebook:

"El tema de la adicción se ha trasladado aquí a la dependencia tecnológica, a las cámaras que registran estos sucesos. Tal es la paradoja de la amistad trash: aun siendo, por defecto, secreta e inconfesable, necesita de un archivo que dé cuenta de sus avatares, y el secreto de ese archivo estará siempre amenazado." Eloy Fernández Porta (*Homo Sampler*)

•

If I were to take any notes in the notebook El Autista gave me, I'd write down the dreams I've had lately:

I dream of snakes, black and fat. Tangled snakes. They open their mouths: rows of fangs like hypodermic needles. They flick their forked tongues: Sssstop . . . we're not Rassstas . . . not Rassstas . . . we're not Rassstas . . . not Rassstas . . . we're not Rassstas . . . not Rassstas . . . we're not Rassstas . . . not Rassstas . . . And like an echo, the organic whispers that come from the depths of a suburban jungle covered in toxic waste intensify: We're not Rassstas . . . not Rassstas . . . we're not Rassstas . . . not Rassstas . . . we're not Rassstas . . . not Rassstas . . . we're not Rassstas . . . not Rassstas . . .

I dream of La Therapist. But that's not the actual dream. Without taking her clothes off, La Therapist becomes blurry and fades little by little. I press the remote control button, but I can't manage to reestablish the hologram. Then I ask myself where the hell we're getting power from in this shitty dump. Then I hear the noise, the terrible noise, and I wake up.

•

La Therapist: Okay, let's forget all this about the *cubensis* and the Paleolithic. Let's . . .

El Autista: The Neolithic, of course. A period associated with the advent of agriculture, sedentary life, and the use of ceramic and polished stone. Of course, some of these features belong to previous periods. In fact, during the Neolithic, these characteristics didn't always come together.

La Therapist: Dios mío.

El Autista: It is important to note that agriculture and the domestication of animals like cows, chickens, goats, and pigs were not the results of a brilliant discovery; they came out of necesidad. Necesidad was one of the many pressures *Homo cubensis* endured.

La Therapist: We're not getting anywhere. I don't have to listen to you.

El Autista: One last thing about Neolithic art, it showcases a great variety of fetishes (mostly female, in case this may be of importance someday), but I would say . . .

La Therapist: No, don't get me involved in this.

El Autista: . . . the greatest achievements of the *Homo cubensis* are found in a series of impressive structures known as Los Monumentos.

La Therapist: Adiós, dulzura.

Noise: Blades and wind from a helicopter over El Vertedero, over our heads. The Rastas run toward the shelter and shout: The weed! They move around, madly, trying to hide it, in a storm of fluorescent leaves and choking snakes. El Autista looks at me with his blank stare and says: The notebooks. (Stacked in a corner and multiplying like malignant cells after radiation exposure.)

Then the soldiers knock down the door, it's not really a door—even a child could have kicked it down. The Rastas lift their arms and fall to their knees. At no point do they stop pointing their weapons at us. One of the soldiers approaches and says: The bones. Hand over the bones.

So, we hand over the skeleton, down to the very last splinter. Then the helicopters leave in the same direction they came from.

Or this:

"We don't have any bones," I tell the soldiers. They search every corner and don't find anything because it's true we no longer have the bones.

They throw picks and shovels at us.

"Start digging."

We start digging right there, El Autista and I, and the two almost identical, almost indistinguishable Rastas. Everything seems to indicate we're digging our own graves.

The tools hit the bones. We unearth them one by one.

With the skeleton duly assembled, inventoried, and placed in a box, the soldiers board their helicopters and leave at once.

"Muchas gracias," they say as they leave.

That's it.

•

El Autista: [. . .] numerous burial mounds of great proportions. The most impressive are called "megaliths:" menhirs, or upright-standing stones. In most cases, they are found isolated, but on occasion, they are in groups, in circles; the anthropomorphic menhir statues placed on enormous tile-covered platforms; the great megalith graves, one of the most renowned is found in the site known as "Plaza de la Revolución." Many of Los Monumentos were profusely decorated with carvings, and the outline of some may very well be related to a worship of the past or to tragic predictions of the future. They are probably the most notable achievement of any human group of the Stone Age. Just to think about the amount of work required for the carving, the transportation, and the erection of the megaliths evokes profound respect for their builders. Builders who were only equipped with inefficient tools and precarious materials.

There it is.

Ladies and gentlemen, the Freeway.

From horizon to horizon. Many kilometers wide. An infinite number of lanes, exit ramps, and multiple levels with seemingly unnecessary loops and complicated intersections.

Even if you had been there from the beginning and watched it come together little by little, it isn't any less impressive.

I have nothing and will always have nothing, but right now, I'd like to have a camera. That tells you something.

•

Cars will soon zoom by. At first, in each direction, only cargo trucks go by, semis. They devour the virgin asphalt with the determination of remote-controlled vehicles. Until, all of a sudden, a truck skids, and a bottle flies out. The bottle lands on the side of the road on a patch of grass. Intact.

•

"Rum and what?" El Autista asks.

"Straight. That's how it ships from the factory."

Neither one of us likes rum, but because it's a miracle the bottle survived, we feel obligated to drink it.

We toast to the future. We quickly get drunk and have double visions about a future that might not have been the future we had initially toasted to.

"What should we do with the empty bottle?" El Autista asks.

"Let's toss it into the sea without a message. Or with a blank message."

"Or with a piece of paper that states: *'Have you ever felt bewildered by or frightened of the female anatomy? Because I have, and I'm the owner.' Signed: Juliette Lewis.*"

"Did she really say that?" All of a sudden, from the top of the bottle, ectoplasm. "What did you do, Juliette Lewis?"

"It was by accident," El Autista says.

A figure condenses in the air: an elderly man in a smoking jacket hovers before us smiling, his lips looking like blown-up balloons.

"Go ahead: three wishes. You know how this goes."

El Autista and I distribute the wishes: one wish each and one that'll make us both happy. (We both know the last one is impossible.)

By accident. That's how I get the camera with a zoom lens and tripod. Too bad it doesn't come with a photographer. It's a shame I wasn't sober enough to think it through and ask for something worthwhile instead.

Something related to the anatomy of celebrities.

El Autista takes his time. He looks at the Freeway. He contemplates.

About ten minutes later, he says:

"I want a car."

•

Idea: a secret bunker where I can examine the pictures I take of the Freeway. In peace. On a computer screen. I'll zoom into the photo's molecular level. What I hold isn't a camera, it's a precision instrument.

•

"You didn't specify," El Genio says.

The car that appeared out of thin air was an ordinary clunker, used and unmarked, with a sloppy paint job and red, white, and blue stripes.

"The colors of the flag," El Autista says. "What a nice gesture."

"What kind of Genio are you?" I ask.

"Roberto, Roberto Goizueta, at your service," the old man says and extends his hand. "Listen, I'm sorry, but I didn't create the wish business. Filling up the tank will cost you at least one wish. Sometimes it'll cost you all three, so you got off easy. What I can do is offer a different kind of fuel. It extends the life of the engine, generates more power, reduces gas consumption and . . . it's much cheaper! You don't need me to get a hold of it. I bet you know what I'm talking about." Excited, the old man examines our exhausted, mute faces. "Nothing? Let's see, young men, think of a black liquid that makes one shout: 'This stuff understands engines and propels cars forward! It is full of magic!' Do you know what it is?"

"No."

"No."

"Really? You don't know?"

We shake our heads wearily.

"Fuck," El Genio says.

•

And without further delay: the cars. The models, the colors, the changes in personality. The blazing chrome devours the virgin asphalt. In just a few hours, the Freeway is flooded with cars. Northbound. Southbound. More and more cars go by, and with each passing one, the speed and distance between them decreases. Until the Freeway—that strip of highway in our audio-visual field—is covered with cars. Cars that barely move. Cars that honk. Cars that advance only a few meters per hour.

•

(stalled.jpg)

It's more than just a sports car. It's body art. It's not the fact that the doors of the animal called Lamborghini Murciélago are open, it's that they're not doors, they're membranous wings. There's a row of fangs between the headlights. Muscles have grown beneath the metal, the swollen body is covered by triangular plates and spikes.

Zoom in: There is a woman inside the beast. Over the wheel, she hides her face between her arms. It isn't necessary to see her face to know she's beautiful, but not one of those beautiful women who until recently drove by in convertibles with hair blowing in the wind. This one is like the supermodel who hides, who runs away, who has made a dangerous bargain. Tired of cursing and asking herself why, why, why she's not getting ahead, she can only hide her face between her arms and throw herself over the wheel of the Lamborghini Murciélago and shine, silently and dazzlingly.

•

"Believe me, I've seen my share of bottlenecks," El Genio de la Botella says. "But this one is the greatest of them all. They must be asking themselves: Where does it begin? Where does it end? What a show. I bet this doesn't come out in the documentary."

"How do you know about the documentary?" I ask him. "Haven't you been stuck in a rum bottle all this time?"

"Yes, but I've been stuck in that bottle because I'm El Genio."

"The filming is over," El Autista informs us. "As soon as the Freeway was completed, they turned off their cameras and left."

"We never really knew who they were," I clarify.

"What the two of you need is a camera . . ." The old man softly looks at me. "A video camera."

"For what?" I ask him.

"So you can film. So you can continue filming. The documentary can't stop now. Not now, this is the good part. What's going to happen with all the movement on the Freeway?"

"Nothing is moving," El Autista says.

"Maybe not right now. But you'll see when the traffic gets going. A freeway changes everything, it transforms everything . . . and who's going to document it? You two: the new directors. You can be the next big stars of independent film."

"Independent film doesn't exist," El Autista says.

"And what are you going to do? Lurk around, take pictures, and jot down notes in your little notebooks? Stay here with your arms crossed when you have before you the continuation, the sublimation, or, better yet, the refutation of the latest documentary? When you can tell the other side of the story, and more importantly, make money doing it? Because, truly, what are your financial prospects in this wasteland? Muchachos, I'm talking about the risk, the opportunity . . . I too, when I had the opportunity, faced the greatest challenge of my life."

"So, what happened?"

•

(15.jpg)

A young man in an Impala alone, reading. The driver's seat is empty. There's a Lexus behind the Impala and a Dodge Magnum in front of it. In the lanes behind: a Subaru, a Taurus, a Hyundai Veracruz, a Toyota Matrix, a BMW, and the rear of what might be a Mitsubishi Diamante. A group of men has gathered between the cars. They all look at the BMW, which is black and has closed, tinted windows. After a few hours, it looks like nobody has gotten out of the BMW, nobody has opened any doors or rolled down any of the windows. As if this weren't enough, the BMW is suspended about fifteen centimeters above the pavement. Just like the ad: *Reality is fifteen centimeters below*. Many emotions—from fear to sexual arousal—merge in the faces of the men who watch the BMW, but one thing is clear: they all want those fifteen centimeters. One of the men is next to the Impala: He looks like the young man's dad. The young man, oblivious to the levitating car, is doing his own thing. Reading a book. It was without a doubt an urgent reading. The pixilation prevents the words from being legible.

•

In 1980, Roberto Goizueta was appointed president of Coca-Cola. A great achievement. A Cuban chemist becomes the first foreigner to lead the most famous brand in the world. But no. The real achievement was yet to come.

Roberto Goizueta had only one thing on his mind: Pepsi.

He saw Pepsi in everything. A sandwich: Pepsi. A leaf falling from a tree: Pepsi. A young woman in a short dress at the park: Pepsi.

Roberto Goizueta decided he had to do something about it. He had to put an end to Pepsi once and for all. If not, he would go mad.

He had an idea. He realized it was The Idea; the only, the definitive, the big one. Maybe he was already mad. He had to talk with El Jefe in private.

"El Jefe" was what they called Robert Woodruff, the owner of the company at the time, the man who brought Coca-Cola to the entire world after World War II. El Jefe was ninety-five years old; he was deaf, blind, and looked like a ghost. He didn't give a damn about anything anymore.

After talking to El Jefe, Roberto Goizueta met with his subordinates. He told them about the future. He was the future. He reminded them he was, above all, a chemist. He told them the only things that existed were chemical formulas, not sacred formulas. He told them the moment to change the formula of Coca-Cola had arrived. He assured them El Jefe was on board with the Change.

But Woodruff died suddenly, right before the launch of New Coke in 1985. He would never see what happened next.

•

(loststill.jpg)

A broken-down Yutong bus on the Freeway. Two passengers leaning out of the window, another one leaning against the door holding a Pepsi. The rest are outside the bus, caught in a variety of poses evoking desolation and weariness. They're fans of an old TV series: *Lost.* South Americans, probably. Compulsive captionists. They were on their way to or heading back from a fan convention when they got stranded in the middle of nowhere. They were still in full costume. There's a Jack, a Sawyer, and a Desmond. There are two Charlies, the rocker, and a Daniel, the quantum physicist, and several who only come close to looking like the terrible Linus. There's an attractive woman who could be either Kate or Juliet. There's even a large woman as Hugo. A mulato, Sayid, looks at me the very instant I take the picture. Then the image begins to move:

"Do you think this is funny, paparazzi?"

The others behind Sayid come forward. La She-Hugo takes a rock from the ground. Naturally, they're annoyed and frustrated. The image is the only thing that moves. Even the wind is still.

"Are you from around here, paparazzi?"

I used to be from here. I was here before the Freeway, before all the stalled cars. But I don't say anything.

One of the Linuses asks me what is happening. I reply with only three words:

"I don't know."

"Get lost."

"Ya."

I step away. After a while, I realize El Autista is walking beside me.

"How long have you been there?" I ask.

"We can't take on the entire Freeway. It's just the two of us."

"Only a few Losties who got a little upset. Nothing to worry about." I tell him, but I'm not sure he understands. He always had a peculiar way of watching television.

"We have to find a video camera. There were cameras everywhere when they were filming the documentary. They probably lost one around here."

"Of course. Where?"

"I don't know."

•

The marketing to promote the new Coca-Cola formula was breathtaking. The consumers, however, did not understand that they were participating in an historic moment.

They only saw a crisis. The Company received hundreds of thousands of phone calls and hundreds of thousands of letters demanding the original formula. Protests and wailing saturated with fanaticism, with stubborn negotiations, with the grief for a motherland that disappears between one's lips:

"I only believe in two things: God and Coca-Cola. Now you have taken one of those things away from me. God only knows what I'm capable of now."

In México, Goizueta's father began receiving death threats from narco addicts, while millions of mothers were giving their children New Coke in baby bottles.

The babies cried.

In La Habana, Fidel Castro crushed old cans with his hands:

"The disappearance of Coca-Cola is a symptom of the fall of US imperialism."

The babies continued to cry.

Not even three months after the launch of New Coke, Goizueta knew he had to return to the original formula.

Coke Classic. Just Coke.

Fuck.

"But I don't regret it. I never have," El Genio says. "New Coke was, and is, the right formula. The one that will destroy Pepsi. Although at that point, it wasn't just about Pepsi but about something that was, and continues to be, beyond any bottle . . . one must do what one must to do."

•

(onewithoutflash.jpg)

The Freeway blisters in the light. The headlights, the blinkers, the light from those very tall pillars look like the masts of a spaceship, a sinking spaceship. And all those people, men, women, and children agape staring at the sky. As if they were looking at much more than the same moon and the same stars. As if they were shocked, their surprised looks captured in a terrifying photo. They will get into their comfortable cars. Most won't survive the night.

•

We walked many kilometers along the bottleneck, with no rush, without any idea where we would find an abandoned camera. They have taken most of the shipping containers, and the ones that are left (the ones that will always remain as part of the landscape) are empty.

"Why don't we use our third wish?" I ask El Autista.

"I used it already. Lo siento."

"What the hell did you ask for?"

"You'll have to see it with your own eyes."

I look at the ground. I discover a sheet of metal covered by vines.

"It looks like a hatch." We open it and go downstairs to what looks like an abandoned bunker. Everything is dark.

Roberto Goizueta? Castro asks, wearing a red-white-and-blue tracksuit. There is no furniture in the office, which is why they're sitting on the floor. It's me, Jefe, Goizueta says. You are El Jefe, Castro replies, smiling. His smile suddenly frightens Goizueta—it reminds him of the way he looked at Woodruff right before his death: like a ghost. I know what you're thinking, Goizueta says. You're thinking about the New Coke fiasco. El Jefe shrugs his shoulders. Don't be so hard on yourself, he says. The truth is that when I nationalized the Coca-Cola plant, I never imagined a fellow countryman would try to turn it into something else right under my nose—and by doing so, terrorize the entire world. I swear that never crossed my mind. But listen: no matter what, we must do what we must do. (And, in parenthesis, Diet Coke turned out alright, didn't it?) Goizueta looks outside, notices the walls have turned into glass. He had the sensation he was in the White House, but what he sees on the other side is Atlanta. At least an Atlanta superimposed on the images of the landscape of La Habana from his childhood. Sugarcoated landscapes. Landscapes defined not so much by the countryside but by the totality of the Habanacampo combo. Until the day I died, murmurs Goizueta. What? El Jefe asks. Until the day I died, I was making New Coke for myself, for my private consumption, Goizueta says. I would have done the same, El Jefe says approvingly. Goizueta observes that the floor is made of glass, the glass is growing colder, and the transparent walls have begun closing in on him, separating him from El Jefe, who is undergoing a similar process of isolation on the other side of the office. Their respective spaces are closing in on them until they can hardly move. Just what I needed, Goizueta says, to end up trapped in a bottle. Can you believe we're genios now? The kind that grant wishes, El Jefe says encouragingly. Must one always grant the wishes of the consumers? Goizueta asks himself. I hope by now people know what to ask for, El Jefe says from inside the bottle in front of him, and adds in a voice that fades away and is gone forever: Goodbye, Jefe, it has been a pleasure talking to you . . . And Goizueta doesn't hear anything else.

•

I film El Autista sharing his opinion about history—History, with a capital H—now that El Genio de la Botella is finally gone:

"It was clearly a good move. A perfect calculation. I'll lose a few million in a few months. But then I'll come back and, because of the product withdrawal, sales will shoot through the roof over the following months. I've got them by the neck."

From inside the camera comes the distorted voice of El Jefe:

"Hmm . . . That's an interesting theory."

•

Rewind:

The recently completed Freeway empties out. The last shots of the documentary: the cameras follow David LaChapelle, who walks around wistfully, waiting for the cars to start passing by.

David LaChapelle:

"I don't have financial issues; I'm a famous photographer. I could stay here forever. I am, of course, afraid of not being on the pop culture radar and of being forgotten. But I also have to change and take this path. I don't want to be fake. I don't want to be that person who makes a bunch of money and doesn't do what they love. At the time, I loved what I used to do. But now, I couldn't shoot the next Britney Spears. I don't care about the next Britney Spears."

El Hall of Fame

Naturally, gas stations, repair shops, cafés, restaurants, motels, and knickknack and souvenir shops are sprouting along the banks of the Freeway. From coast to coast. A fringe of civilization, an insulating strip between the Freeway and the desert.

We all win.

•

El Autista and I find fast work in fast food. For now, since it's a new business, we're the only employees. It goes without saying we don't know what we're doing.

"It looks like you're a couple of hard workers," the owner tells us. "Do you like baseball? Everyone knows me as El Pitcher."

The place is decorated with posters of famous baseball players, medals, trophies, banners, emblems of different teams, uniforms, and game equipment. It's the décor for the grand opening, the first pitch, but it looks more like a department store than a restaurant.

The neon sign outside was supposed to read EL PITCHER FRITO, but due to an error or a lack of funds or for some other reason we're unaware of, the Ts are missing. The neon sign reads: EL PICHER FRIO/ABIERTO LAS 24 HORAS.

In the restaurant parking lot, we set the camera down in front of the car. All of a sudden, the car wakes up. Its headlights are big eyes that blink:

"What are you planning on doing?" it asks.

Meanwhile, El Pícher Frío shows up:

"I was looking for you . . . um, a car that talks? How is that possible?"

"Don't ask me," the car says. It closes its eyes again.

"It's . . . alive? How is that possible?" El Pícher Frío asks again.

"I asked El Genio for a wish," El Autista explains.

"No, it can't be."

"It's true," I confirm. "It was our third wish."

"Genios don't exist. Neither does magic. Fantasy isn't real."

"Maybe not," El Autista admits.

"But there it is. Incredible . . . look, I'm frozen in shock."

"In this heat?" the car murmured. "Now, that's incredible."

•

It's absurd to think many famous people will set foot in this restaurant. Not as absurd as to think that, once in a while and when you least expect it, *someone* will get out of their car and eat fries with ketchup before continuing on their way. And here I'll be, ready to identify the customers we need for the documentary, like a coolhunter. Hunting interesting people who may want to talk to us, and then we edit. (It's best if they're not baseball players.)

The autistic version, the local version of the coolhunter: Do what you can with what you find first.

Something like this:

"Excuse me, sir. Would you be willing to talk to us a little bit about the Freeway? Or, if you prefer, about anything else?"

And all of a sudden, the man, whose name is Christopher Arendt, a gray-haired guy, worn-out, looks up from his food, chews a little bit, ruminant, cautiously, thoughtfully, and says:

"I've barely been here ten minutes, and I'm already thinking about Guantánamo."

El Autista motions for me to bring the camera to the table.

•

I liked working night shifts, because whenever they were awake, I wanted to apologize to them. When they were sleeping, I didn't have to worry about that. I could just walk up and down the blocks all night long.

There was usually one detainee who would lead the call to prayer at five in the morning. That person was in the very last cell. The detainees, they sang beautifully. All the detainees would get up in the morning and, in unison, sing this gorgeous song that I could never understand and that still rings in my ears. It was so eerie to hear.

Have you heard of Camp Delta? Camp Delta is on a cliff that overlooks the ocean. I had never been to the ocean before in my whole life. I grew up in Michigan, in a trailer, in the middle of a cornfield. The beauty I found there, in Camp Delta, was way out of my range of possibility.

Every day you walked down the blocks, forty-eight people in two rows of twenty-four cells, and you have no idea what any of them are there for. They're just sitting in their cells. You give them food, and if they get crazy, you spray them with this terrible oil-based chemical. Then you send these five guys in to beat the shit out of them.

I had bought enough porn before I left for Cuba. I ended up cutting them up, and I put the remnants of the pornos and DVD covers all over my wall. I made a wallpaper on my half of the room. My mom sent me a packet of dinosaur stickers, so all of the particularly obscene shots I covered with dinosaurs. Asses, vaginas, nipples . . . I would just sit and contemplate the dinosaurs for hours.

I tied a cord to the ceiling fan that was in my room and I tried to hang myself, but I ripped the fan out of the ceiling. That was about two months before we went home.

Is there anything I miss? I miss the cups. The detainees were only allowed to have Styrofoam cups, and they would write and draw all over them. I'm not totally familiar with their culture, but they never drew the human form. And of course, I never understood what they wrote. They were like strange works of art, very condensed; the writing and the drawings would literally cover the entire cup. Then we would have to take them. It was a ridiculous process. We would take the cups and send them to our military intelligence. They would just look at these things and then throw them away. I used to love those little cups.

•

El Pícher Frío pants. He looks dizzy. I realize now how much he looks like Christopher Arendt. El Autista will later share that he thinks they're more or less the same person.

El Pícher Frío offers Christopher Arendt a Happy Meal to go. He walks around the place. Instinctually, Christopher checks the bag.

"The toy's missing. The Happy Meal comes with a toy."

"We're out. I'm so sorry. Would you take a signed baseball?"

". . ."

. . . and Christopher Arendt gets back on the Freeway, and El Pícher Frío asks us to turn the camera off. We had already turned it off. We saw it coming. A few seconds later, he breaks the ice. Turns out, he had also been at Guantánamo.

•

Since the documentary is about a freeway, El Autista thought it would be best to tell the story from a car's perspective.

The car says:

"I don't have any perspective. Look at me. I'm stranded in a parking lot under a brutal sun. A sun that beats you down. A sun that seizes you like a meteorite engulfed in flames. A sun that makes you loathe yourself. My eyes are made of plastic, which is why I can look at it head-on and have seen how much it enjoys it. Sadistic sun. Full sun. Sinister total sun. Have you ever asked yourselves why they put this infernal sun over you? What did you do to deserve such a punishment? That's what I'd like to know. Bring me buckets of water. Lots of buckets of water. Better yet, bring me buckets of chicken. I can fry all the chicken you want on my hood."

I ask El Autista if this is the perspective we needed.

He remembers training. It lasted forever. When he was pitching, he would sometimes forget about himself and about his arm. He couldn't even feel the ball in the palm of his hand. Everything would disappear, even the damn ball. Nothing else existed beyond the catcher squatting across from him, who he would see as an annoying spot in his field of vision, a blurry outline. Every so often, a cough or sarcastic comment behind him would make the shadows of the pitching coaches on the turf reappear. Then a saving voice would come on the speaker:

"How many pitches do you have?"

"Twelve thousand five hundred forty-three."

"Perfect. Prepare for questioning."

Later, in his room, his body, the body of a high-performing athlete, was no more than a padded bulge, a mattress falling on another mattress: to sleep, to sleep . . . restorative thoughts. And his mind would drag through the halls and reach the dining hall, his favorite place, everyone's favorite place. The next day, they would be there, waiting for the high-calorie broths, the energy shakes . . . Yes, the food was good at Guantánamo, you can't deny that it was plentiful and good. Although he could never shake the vague feeling that the food was missing something, I don't know, it was always missing *something*.

•

A suspicious character in a grotesque disguise enters the restaurant. It's clear he doesn't want to be recognized. A white mask covers his face. On his head a Kentucky Fried Chicken bucket and a sticker across it with the word FUNERAL. I think he must be an artist. I think he must be a musician. I think: progressive metal, thrash metal, funk, electronica, jazz, bluegrass, avant-garde. All that.

•

Luckily, hitting wasn't his thing. Although, in the end, he couldn't say which was worse.

There was a bat made of solid lead that caused herniated disks and would dislocate both shoulders when swung. There was a bone density bat that would break easily. Every bat you broke cost you a broken bone—that would teach you not to break what belonged to the team, in other words, what belonged to everybody. But at batting practice, the one his teammates feared the most was a nunchaku bat.

A standard bat apparently, but once swung, that piece of Asian equipment would break into two halves connected by a chain. Depending on the chain's length, the upper half would hit the batter's head, back, abdomen, or ribs. A longer chain might wrap around his neck. Practice would become that much more brutal because there was no way to tell a standard bat from a nunchaku bat—you didn't know if it would split midswing. When you didn't think it would, you ended up hitting yourself using your own strength. When you thought it would split, you would swing slowly in a ridiculous fashion and shrivel like a frightened animal, but then the bat turned out to be a standard one. And, of course, you would never hit the ball.

A different method, less violent but equally baffling, was internalized hitting. Instead of bats, we used brooms, canes, umbrellas, fishing rods, butterfly nets . . . swing after swing, the batter would listen to a recording of laughter. A recording of his teammates' laughter.

There was outdoor training and there was the gym, where it was mandatory to be naked. An optical device installed in the walls would make some penises look smaller. The shrinking effect was random, on a scale from life-size to microscopic, and it only affected one in ten penises, never any more than that. They would all look at each other as they lifted weights, comparing the proportions of other penises to their own.

But not everything was about physical appearance. Every morning, they engaged in activities that would invariably include phrases such as "we, Cuban baseball players," and invariably ended with pledges.

•

Buckethead says:

"I am Buckethead. I was raised by chickens in a coop. When I was younger, I performed puppet shows on corners until I bought my first guitar. I explain all this in one of the songs of my fifth album, *Monsters and Robots*. My mission in life is to alert the world to the ongoing chicken holocaust in fast-food joints around the globe. Here I am."

"The Holocaust already happened here," El Autista murmurs as he walks by, bringing imitation Big Macs to another table. He has told everybody that the burgers are made from human meat. El Pícher Frío doesn't know that's why his sales are so high, the reason why customers are taking tons of burgers to go.

"Fried chicken. Will there be anything else?" I ask, ready to write down the order. But instead of looking at the menu, Buckethead notices the restaurant's baseball theme.

"I'm curious. Why 'El Pícher Frío'?"

"Because the owner used to be a pitcher."

"Does he pitch scoops of ice cream?"

•

He recalls a few friends. Alexander, who as a boy swore he would never play baseball. Tito Barba, known as El Psicópata of Santa Cruz del Sur. Then there's Cabrerita, from Ciénaga in Matanzas, who humbly rejected million-dollar offers from the Yankees and White Sox: "I'm not that good. Any one of you is better," he would say. "Besides, what am I going to do with all that money?"

Not all of his friends were pitchers, although he was forced to spend more time with the other pitchers. Once, while warming up, they began to discuss the origin of the term *bullpen*:

Bull means *toro*; *pen*, *corral*. Basic English. The bullpen is where the bulls wait before being let into the bullring. The bullpen is where the bulls wait before being driven to the slaughterhouse. Etcetera. Then they began to pitch curved interpretations: the corral could refer to a cage, or a cell, or a combination (*pen*), and the bull represents the guard—this supported the idea that prison guards tended to have bull-like features: they're large, robust, and ill-tempered . . . Then the topic of Japanese Americans in World War II came up. After Pearl Harbor, the US government gathered all the Japanese from the West Coast and relocated them to makeshift internment camps throughout the country. The pitchers did not know their history well: that was a fast fact; nobody knew where it came from, a subliminal breeze that suddenly blew through the field, carrying voices. Voices that muttered a dissonant and not-so-basic English, the English of the Big Leagues. Among them, the voice of a survivor of a camp on the California-Oregon border:

"Prisoners in the military prison lived in wooden buildings which offered some protection from severe winters. However, prisoners in the *bullpen* were housed outdoors in tents without heat and with no protection against the bitter cold. For the first time in our lives, those of us confined to the *bullpen* experienced a life and death struggle for survival . . ."

And when they warmed up, just talking for the sake of talking, the pitchers recalled a certain William "Big Bill" Haywood, the one-eyed union activist from Salt Lake City who without a doubt would have made a magnificent baseball player. But in the mines and strikes and confrontations with the police, he learned socialism instead of baseball.

Bill—"I've-never-read-Marx's-*Capital*-but-I-have-the-marks-of-capital-all-over-me"—Haywood, who died depressed and lonely in Moscow, assassinated by alcohol and diabetes, longing to return to the Labor Union in the States. Old Big Bill, whose autobiography the pitchers read (at Guantánamo the pitchers would read) about the strikes and the miners in Idaho who passed "months of imprisonment in the *bullpen,* a structure unfit to house cattle, enclosed in a high barbed wire fence." Another well-read book was *Roughneck: The Life and Times of Big Bill Haywood,* by biographer Peter Carlson, in which he writes: "Haywood traveled to the town of Mullan, where he met a man who had escaped from the *bull-pen.*" The discussion about a single word turned into speculation about the possibility of escape. Then they all took their balls and went off to pitch.

One day, they began to smuggle autographed balls to each other. The idea was to sign as many as they could, write "Guantánamo" and the date beside the signature—it was all illegible. The player who did not have an irreversibly injured arm would pitch the balls as far as he could, over the tall barbed wire fence. And although many were discovered and confiscated by the coaches before they could be pitched, they pitched quite a few of those inked balls, which could not fit one more autograph, into the Guantánamo desert . . .

He also recalls Maykel, who said he would quit if he could sell hot dogs at the World Series. The Arroyo brothers, who were like two steroid-enlarged güijes. There was

Ráfaga, the last exportable product from Nueva Gerona. Ah, and how can one forget Yusnavy Izquierdo, the wonder boy.

•

Seems like Buckethead hasn't come by to eat. He's not interested in ordering anything. I ask him if he would like a Happy Meal. He says he's not interested.

"But I'll take the toy as a souvenir. Bring me the toy."

"We don't have toys here," I tell him.

"Then it's not a real Happy Meal. Just like what you're doing isn't a real documentary."

He must have seen the camera somewhere.

"Would you mind sharing a few words. To mark your visit?"

"I was in an actual documentary once. *American Music: Off the Record*. But I didn't say a single word; I came out playing. That's what I can do for you, the restaurant, and perhaps for this rural isle. Play."

"Off the record," I confirm.

•

Among the ghosts of the past, Yusnavy Izquierdo:

The guy was an anomaly. He played all the diamond positions well. He ran like an Olympic sprinter. He could hit home runs from either side of the plate. His career had followed a migratory path. Born nearby, in Caimanera, a small town in the province of Guantánamo, from which he had enough sense to escape quickly, he played with Santiago in the youth conference, and then immediately moved to La Habana. His National Series debut was with Los Industriales, and he was named Rookie of the Year. The following year he was back at Guantánamo. Escaping would be more difficult this time.

But he tried.

"Yusvany asked me to break out with him," El Pícher Frío tells us. "He had a plan. He had studied the base's facilities. He memorized the duct system. We just had to dig to expand the diameter of one of the tunnels so we would be able to fit through. Are you sure that'll take us outside? I asked. Totally sure, he told me. But what are we going to do once we're out? I asked. We move, he said, I'll guide you. I know Oriente as well as if I had maps of it tattooed on my body. We can hide in los montes, in los pueblos . . . You're crazy, Yus, I said. What pueblos are you talking about? He was still optimistic, imagining the infinite possibilities of the other side. I could see nothing but the wild desert in which we were going to die scorched by the sun. I told him not to count on me. But the son of a bitch was convincing and charismatic. We started digging with patience and determination, day after day, from vent to vent, taking advantage of our free time until our bodies gave out."

Sometime later, the two of them reached the projected

distance. They dragged themselves through the tunnel for kilometers and kilometers, tunneling through the last few meters, on the verge of fainting. With their arms and legs bleeding, they emerged onto the field of pruned grass. A group of coaches and doctors were waiting for them. On the horizon, farther beyond, there was another row of barbed wire. The sports complex was much bigger than Yusnavy had imagined. On the field, there were other holes similar to the one they had made to break through to the surface; there were other tunnels that also ended there through which on previous occasions their teammates had tried to escape. The coaches and doctors congratulated them. He and Yusnavy had completed the most dramatic exercise imaginable, which demonstrated that they were baseball players capable of great heroism.

They let themselves collapse onto the stretchers the doctors had ready. Before losing consciousness, El Pícher Frío heard that voice:

How many?

Two. They just came out.

Take them to isolation.

•

Buckethead plugs in his guitar and begins to play. The music infuses the restaurant space with something different. A strange ferocity. Everyone there forgets about the crap they're eating. It's the kind of music that says to everyone: Yes, I'm Buckethead. It's the kind of music that says: Buckethead is in the top ten when it comes to the electric guitar. It's the kind of music that says: "He plays like a motherfucker" (Ozzy Osbourne).

All of a sudden, there's a shift. Buckethead's music drifts into a darker space. There, where his alter ego, his anagram, lives: Death Cube K. The being who stalks Buckethead and appears in his nightmares. His other side. His photographic negative. Buckethead hits the chords, and his white mask turns into Death Cube K's black mask. The riffs wander away from the holocaust of fast food. Now it's the kind of music that inspired William Gibson, in whose novel *Idoru* there is a bar called Death Cube K. It's the kind of music that says: we're in a bar very far away from here, be careful—Kafka's Tokyo.

•

"After the escape plan failed," El Pícher Frío tells us, "Yusnavy fell into a severe depression that shortly gave way to the most abnormal joy. What's wrong, Yus? I asked him, irritated by seeing him so happy all the time. We're going to get out of here, he told me. When? I got excited. I don't know when, but someday, he said, the point is we'll get out. Then I asked him how he could be so sure about that, and he explained to me that he had seen the future, or rather, that he had *been* in the future. Not once, but several times. I don't know what happened, he told me, I must have been so depressed that I entered an altered state of consciousness, and that triggered my mind to wander through time. Now you've really lost it, Navy, I said. It can't be, time travel isn't possible. I've done it, he argued, but I can't control it, it comes and goes, and it takes me to the future. But how? How is it possible? I insisted. I felt it was my duty to directly point out to him the absurdity of what he was describing. In the end, I was just jealous. He looked so happy, and I wanted to expose him, I wanted to break him. Okay, explain this, how is it possible only your mind can go there? And what is your body doing in the meantime? It stays back in el campo? But the son of a bitch would shrug his shoulders and say: All I know is that I have traveled through time even if you don't think it's possible, I don't care about anything else. I started to get really annoyed. I shouted: Time travel is pure fantasy! How can you talk about fantasy and science fiction bullshit after all we've experienced? Mierda. So that's how you plan to escape now? Cojones, esto es la realidad. Maybe I was too harsh on him, but I needed Yusnavy back, to stay with me in the intolerable present, resisting. I was scared. I remember that he hugged me and said: I can't tell you much because they're always listening here, but I'm going to say two things from survivor to survivor: One, you and I will leave sooner or later; two, I'm going to play in the Japanese League because, based on what I saw, that's where it's all going to be and the car. They've talked almost every night. I worry. I ask him what they have talked about, but El Pícher Frío doesn't respond. He remains silent, and that was the last time I saw him: still alive, eyes closed, thinking about the toys he'll never have, murmuring to himself: that car . . . that car . . .

•

We find him the next day. In the meat locker.

"Come see this," El Autista says to me. I go over and find him hanging from the neck, hanging like a frozen piece of meat.

He was wearing his baseball uniform. He was even wearing his glove.

El Autista is wearing a leather coat, hat, thick boots, and two pairs of pants—one on top of the other. He bundles up like an Eskimo every time he goes into the meat locker, even if it's for a second.

"What do we do now?" El Autista asks me as he touches the inert body, swinging it.

"What are you trying to say?"

•

Art Spiegelman, or someone passing as Art Spiegelman, or someone who thinks he is Art Spiegelman, is still chewing on pieces of himself when the camera approaches:

La XXX

What La Habana once was. What it never was. Whatever it might have been. The Freeway has wiped her off the map. In her place, the endless asphalt that fills our nightmares. But we're working on a movie. We have a restaurant. We wait, every second, for a stroke of luck.

•

One day, a mysterious visitor comes inside:

"Would you like to sell this place, muchachos?"

"Who are you?" I ask.

"I go by Santos. I'm with the Miami Mafia." He places a black briefcase on the table, opens it. It's packed with wads of one-hundred-dollar bills. "Considering how things are going at the ranch, it's a lot of money. You can take it and get out of here. Or you can stay and work for us and double the amount in a few months. Think about it."

And we think about it.

The only thing I think about is securing a location to continue filming *Lo Que Aparezca*.

El Autista says:

"We're staying."

"Whatever you want. Sign here."

"What are you going to do with the restaurant?"

"It'll no longer be a restaurant, por supuesto. We'll set up a storefront to hide the game room in the back."

Now Santos puts a small box on the table, opens it. There is an earthworm inside. "This is Lansky, a member of a worm species we protect." He takes the earthworm in his hand. "They farm them somewhere in a remote place, over by Poland, Lithuania, or Belarus, nobody really knows, and then they send them to us. Look, this one, which is one of the older ones, still carries a little Communist dirt." He pets the worm with the side of his finger. "Tell me, Lansky, what kind of business are we going to start here? Remember, it has to be something that doesn't attract too much attention in these parts. A discreet place . . . Santos brings the worm to his ear. "What did you say? What was that? Okay, Lansky Lombrizky, if that's what you want. What should we call the sex shop? Let's see, what do you think we should call it?" Santos looks at us and smiles. "Je, je. Are you listening to this?"

•

The fast-food joint that once nourished us quickly becomes a sex shop called La Gusanera.

•

"Martínez Junior, a pleasure," he says, extending his hand. The other representative of the Miami Mafia: a gray-haired, stocky guy holding a habano cigar and wearing fifteen gold chains. "Autista, eh?"

"Yes, but no," El Autista says.

"It's a nickname," I clarify.

"But it's a nickname for a reason, no? Perhaps because you have special abilities, like an extraordinary memory or the ability to do complex calculations. Because you're a great observer and have superconcentration. Perfect. You come with us to the game room. Your job will be to supervise, count chips, count cards, watch roulette, discover geometric patterns in dice rolls, detect beads of sweat on the players' foreheads. I'm still not sure, but I get the sense that you'll be useful at catching cheats and spies." Martínez Jr. immediately looks at me. "You'll be in charge of the shop. You don't know anything about any game room unless they tell you the password. The password is 'I come to play illegally.' Ah, and you also have to do the peep show. We don't have anybody else."

"But I'm not a stripper," I say.

He hands me a worn book.

"Unlikely," he utters. "implausible, atypical . . . Santos, cojones, put that worm down."

The book is *Candy Girl: A Year in the Life of an Unlikely Stripper* by Diablo Cody.

"What am I supposed to do with this?"

"Read it," he says.

•

Inventory:

Adult books and magazines. Adult movies (this documentary). A variety of vibrators. Penises and vaginas. Smoking lingerie. S&M accessories. Costumes. Consoles for virtual sex. Hormones. Adult dolls. Adult food. Dushku Cereal. Etcetera.

Inventory:

For the grand opening, they had promised to bring "the biggest porn star in the world." We imagined a calibrated and exquisite beast, a devil in a woman's body. But when opening day came, they showed up with another man. A very ordinary man, not even a touch of glamour. No mafioso, no cubano-americano. Santos and Martínez Jr. introduce him as Spencer Elden. Yes, the biggest porn star in the world.

•

Spencer Elden was a newborn baby when they took the picture. A baby they photographed naked, underwater, floating. In the picture, there's a fishing hook with a dollar bill for bait. It was an album cover. It was the album with the right song at the right time: "Smells Like—'I was trying to write the ultimate pop song' (Kurt Cobain)—Teen Spirit." An album that sold—"No album in recent history had such an overpowering impact on a generation and such a catastrophic effect on its main creator" (*Rolling Stone*)—thousands of millions of copies. The album was *Nevermind*.

•

My days at La Gusanera:

Standing behind the counter, I have Dushku Cereal with milk for breakfast. Dushku Cereal contains mixed clumps of distinct genetic origin. They're tasty and very nutritious. On the box, there's a two-headed black eagle on a red background. You don't need to know much about cereals to know this is the bicephalous eagle of the Albanian flag.

Later, I go to work in the peep show booth. I get up on the stage and start reading Diablo Cody's book. The customers go into the booths, insert their coins to open their respective windows, and watch me read. I take off my clothes, barely moving, I try my best to turn the pages sensually. A little while later, the men start to masturbate. I know this because I have to replenish toilet paper rolls in the booths at the end of the day. In some, I find semen on the walls and floor, but never very much. I'm not a great attraction; the only thing I do is read. I suppose some are aroused by watching me read in there, while others are aroused by the book I'm reading. It's exhausting because the room is dimly lit, as is appropriate for an erotic show. Even still, sensually and slowly, I continue to read. *Candy Girl: A Year in the Life of an Unlikely Stripper* is one of those books that came out of a blog. Diablo Cody had already documented her experiences as a stripper in the Midwest on her blog *Pussy Ranch*. The possibility of documenting my experience as the reader of *Candy Girl: A Year in the Life of an Unlikely Stripper* under the gaze of the masturbators of La Post-Habana crosses my mind. Diablo herself—a highly trained animal who climbed from the pole to writing and producing for film and TV—could use footage of me reading her book from the security cameras. She could use my blog *Pussy Ranch 2.0: Pero yo no soy una stripper*. She could even take the documentary's autistic concept (in case something like that even existed) and transform it into something else. Into something much more lucrative.

•

My days in La Gusanera:

Most of the time, the worm keeps me company. Lansky crawls through the shop, climbs the shelves, looks for dirt that doesn't exist. But that doesn't stop him from eating. He has grown and fattened up considerably on milk and Dushku Cereal. Floppy, segmented, translucent at times, he looks like an extraterrestrial penis. The customers tend to think it's a kind of bionic product, part dildo, part house pet. Both men and women have tried to purchase him.

Every so often, El Autista pulls out of the game room to see me at the register. He gives me security camera footage. Stealthily, of course, so those very cameras don't record him. The mafiosos are obsessed with the security cameras. They put them all over the shop, and in the back, El Autista has told me, they have a row of monitors. They see everything but they continue to see nothing, he said. They're focused on poker games, bets, chance . . .

Speaking of game vision, El Autista gives me an update on how it's going for Spencer Elden, our Special Guest Star.

•

The other players (some are regulars, mafioso friends of Santos and Martínez Jr., others are travelers, somber and laconic, a pathetic parade of cubano-americanos who are neither cubano nor americano) would come and go. The only one who remained was Spencer. He would: Bet. Lose. Bet again. Lose again. Take a shot. Wait a while. Cry. Laugh. Ask to borrow money. Order a drink. Start all over again. For several days and nights in a row. El Autista deduced it wasn't going to end well. He decided to get something out of Spencer before his celebrity faded completely. El Autista approached Spencer and told him he wanted an interview.

Spencer, sprawled on the floor, barely looked up, and, with an alcohol-induced look, asked: Who are you?

La MTV, responded El Autista. I am the closest thing to La MTV on this ranch.

Where am I?

El Autista splashed water on his face.

I'm underwater, Spencer said.

No, no you're not, El Autista told him.

I've been underwater my entire life, Spencer insisted. It's not a childhood trauma—I want that to be clear. I don't remember anything; I was only a baby.

Of course, El Autista said. You were a sexy baby, naked underwater.

Spencer nodded, sighed. Yes, that image took on a life of its own, and he grew up along with it; their lives started together. He saw the image covering walls and folders. He saw it on hundreds of shirts. He saw it on thousands of magazine covers. He saw it projected on the sky. He learned how to spot it everywhere he went, parodied and manipulated and consumed ad infinitum. Then he realized it was an album cover, and that that baby, so well known everywhere, perhaps the most famous baby in the world, was him. It had been him. And it had been a while since Cobain shot himself in the head.

In Spencer's head, the embedded image developed into a tumor. As a teenager, he would see himself floating underwater, swimming, trying to grab the dollar bill on the hook. While walking, eating, watching La MTV, doing whatever he was doing, the sensation of being submerged assaulted him—in fact, with every movement, he felt the water's resistance, and his vision would become blurry. The dollar bill was the only thing he could ever make out. The dollar bill would appear everywhere, regardless of what was in his field of vision, and he couldn't avoid swimming toward it. Under the water, the dollar bill on the hook. That's it. The hook didn't bother him, even though he knew it was there for a reason. Perhaps the impulse didn't have much to do with going after the actual dollar bill, but with getting caught by the hook, so that he could come out of the water. Regardless, he could never reach the dollar bill nor the hook. The target, so near, yet so far. Swimming in a still image. And, of course, he couldn't breathe.

The worst part of these trances wasn't the sensation of drowning. It wasn't the inability to get out of the water. It wasn't the inability to stop reaching for the dollar bill.

The worst part was being naked. The worst part was knowing that everyone was looking at him. Sensing all those eyes on his penis.

Until one day, he decided to rebel. To give them what they wanted. He was an adult now; he could make his own decisions about his body. He went to a plastic surgeon and underwent a very expensive operation: penis reduction.

He turned himself into a man with a baby's penis.

He turned his penis into a little worm and undressed for the photographers.

I did what I had to do, said Spencer Elden. Can you see it?

•

Bad luck, announced Martínez Jr. Game over.

Spencer asked for one more day, one more chance . . .

No, we've already given you too many chances. The last one was bringing you here. Now we're going for a walk.

We'll be back in a little while, Santos told El Autista. We'll escort the porn star back to the Freeway. We don't want him to get into an accident.

They went out back. They got into the truck. The three of them knew where they were going. What they didn't realize was that El Autista had bugged Spencer.

The truck drove away from the Freeway. It took a dirt road behind the sex shop.

(Spencer.) *I swear to you, I'll do anything, anything . . .*

(Santos.) *What you had to do was pay your debts. You didn't do it.*

The truck drove around on uneven ground. Crushed rocks. The sounds of other cars faded away. Leaving the Freeway behind as they approached the desert.

They stopped.

They took Spencer out of the car.

(Martínez Jr.) *There was always something about you, mi socio. Ever since the record company saw the photo. They were worried about showing your little dick, the same one you have now, the one you've always had, right?* (Laughter.) *Well, they had an alternative cover that didn't show it, but the lead singer . . .*

What was his name, the one who later committed suicide? Kurt Cobain. He refused to change anything about it. I suppose you already knew that. (Silence.) *What I'm trying to tell you is that, if you want, and this is the last thing we're going to do for you, and we've already done more for you than you can imagine, if you want, you can shoot yourself in the head. You can pretend to be Cobain and do what he did. You can think of it as your chance to shoot him, to get rid of him forever. Take it as something you've earned, something worth much more than money. Go ahead. Don't be shy, Elden. My favorite color is red.* (A long silence.)

A gunshot.

They dig.

•

We act as if nothing had happened. Everything remains the same in the shop. The peep show, the illicit games, they all continue. Until the moment I realize something.

El Autista.

It's been a while since I've seen El Autista.

I go to the back. I knock on the door. The door is unlocked. I go inside. There is nobody in the game room. I would have seen them if they had gone out the front door. If they had gone back to the desert again . . . why aren't they here? I go through drawers. There are a bunch of files, classified files, ratings with several Xs: one, two, three . . . There's a poster on the wall. MTV: MIAMI TELEVISION. I close the door, return to the register, and start counting bills. I guess I'm in charge of the shop now.

My days at La Gusanera are numbered.

•

I'm having breakfast when she arrives.

•

I shudder when I see her.

"You're the dead woman," I say. "You're the Miami Mafia."

"There's a *Miami* Mafia? That's the most ridiculous thing I've ever heard in my life."

•

I shudder when I see her.

"Did you come to kill me? The Miami Mafia sent you."

"No, cariño. I'm from Boston," she says. I sigh with relief. "Shouldn't you card me before I come in? How do you know I'm not underage?"

"I bet you're a sexy baby when you're naked."

"Easy, pervert. I'm not even young enough to be a cheerleader anymore. The age I used to be, or that I pretended to be, in the series and movies of the past . . . My teen spirit is dead and buried."

I'm having my cereal when she arrives. She takes Lansky and puts him in her mouth. First, she samples him. She sucks on him slowly. She shoves him down her throat. Then she bites him, ripping him in half. She chews him slowly and looks at me, smiling. She swallows and eats the second half. "Delicious. How much do I owe you?" It wasn't for sale, I tell her. It wasn't even edible. "Oh, I'm sorry," she says. "It's just that I've spent all night driving. I was hungry. I haven't had breakfast. And it looked so . . ."

•

I'm having breakfast when she approaches the register. She has a movie in her hand. I don't read the title. The promotional caption says: "Fuck the cheerleader, fuck the world."

•

She approaches the cereal box. The box is already empty. She's not carrying a movie. It's a business card. On the card: BOSTON DIVA.

"That's my production company."

"And you?" I ask.

"Eliza," she introduces herself. "Eliza Dushku."

"I know who you are. I knew it when you first came in. Question: What are you doing here?"

"Business," she says. Smacking her gum. "There are rumors you're cooking up something good in these parts."

"Rumors"

"Yes."

"About a movie."

"I hope so."

"That you're interested in producing."

"I *might* be interested."

"I'm glad."

"You're glad?"

"I'm glad for you."

"Have you heard any of these rumors?"

"No. My job is to manage this shop."

"I see." Eliza Dushku smiles. I can see her teeth. She makes a provocative gesture with her lips, and, for an instant, I can see her tongue. In fact, I can see her chewing gum. The little white mass between her teeth. "Do you need my help?"

•

Who doesn't?

Everybody needs an actress.

•

I show Eliza Dushku the stage where I read Diablo Cody's book.

"I don't need it," she tells me. "I know perfectly well how to do it without a manual."

I have no doubt about that.

"That's the least I can do after having eaten your worm."

"It wasn't my worm."

"I knew you were going to say that." Eliza Dushku undoes her belt, pulls her zipper down, her jeans slide down her hips. "Watch and learn."

•

She prefers a different method. Private dance: only one observer. It's better to focus movements toward one specific booth. She also wants audio, so the customer can watch and also *hear* what she is going to say.

In her bikini, she climbs the vertical pole; her body grips it perfectly. As if she had been doing this her entire life. The customer glues his face to the peephole; he will probably smash his nose against the glass (some will leave bloodstains on the glass before completely collapsing in the booth). She whispers: Hola, cariño. I'm a baby doll. I'm *your* baby doll.

And the idea begins to develop. She talks about spending her childhood in a dollhouse. She was a small baby doll who played with dolls and then she grew up and became a nice, big baby doll. Your baby doll now. Her private dance is accompanied by intimate stories and memories of armoires and lace. It doesn't take long before the customer has the first of a long series of extreme ejaculations.

And she talks about the day she received a phone call. Hello, Eliza? Yes, this is she, who's this? This is the president. Which president? she asked, distracted, covering her thighs with lotion, rubbing them until they were shiny. The president of Albania. I'm calling to extend a formal invitation. In Albania, we are very eager for you to come and explore your roots.

Her father, Philip Dushku, was Albanian American. She packed her bags.

The president was waiting for her at the airport. They took her to the most luxurious hotel in Tirana, to a suite where she had a huge bed all to herself, with delicious sheets against which she could rub like a naughty baby doll. Just like that, cariño, just like that. On those sheets, I soak in the semen you give me. And her dance moves into a baby doll's private space in the Albanian hotel suite. The intimacy of the bathroom—because she, too, must sit on the toilet to urinate a liquid similar to urine and shower off the excessive material that makes up her skin and her beautiful hair, which of course are real. With her hair brushed, it's time to go to bed. She curls up, satisfied, with the TV on a channel that reports news on the permanent crisis in some savage language.

She went to visit her father's family. She spent time with friends and neighbors. She talked to the people, she asked them to tell stories and share local traditions. A journalist told her the Communist Party there had held on to Stalinism even after the Soviets abandoned it. How interesting, she remarked. She enjoyed the scenery, the connection with the land of her ancestors. She took pictures in the mountains.

She went to Kosovo. She spoke to women who had been in refugee camps, with men who remembered the bombings as if they had happened yesterday. She saw scars she never imagined were possible. She saw mutilated individuals. She spent the night with an old paramilitary soldier who enjoyed being whipped and who lay on the floor like a rug so that she could walk on his back in her stilettos. She had a threesome with two attractive UN soldiers. Her pelvic motor was going at full speed. Her metal skeleton with highly flexible joints took on many positions. Look how far I can to open my legs. You like this, right? I can see how much you like it. I can stretch and bend and twist for you. You can do whatever you want with me. And I also do it with women.

In Kosovo, she met a woman who worked for Human Rights Watch. I've been watching you since you arrived, the HRW lady told her. You're the baby doll I dreamed about as a little girl. You're so . . . realistic. Is this silicone or something far superior? the lady asked, stroking her and licking her on the inside and out. You are the observer, she responded. What do you think?

An entourage of functionaries followed her everywhere. At times she managed to slip away and walk alone, incognito, through ghost towns where there were always power shortages. That's how she met a group of guys who spent all their time drinking and smoking in a garage. She didn't understand a word they said, but she had a great time with them. They washed auto parts and threw suds at each other. In a bikini, draped across the hood of the car, she let them drench her with smuggled gas. Hopefully, the president won't find out about this, she laughed. Then she put her hands on the skimpy bikini. To take it off. Yes, cariño, this bikini I'm wearing. Are you dying for me to take it off? Are you about to come again? Come on, come with me. She was now naked in front of those poor Balkan guys and said: You can bring a match over because this body is fireproof.

There she is. Naked on the stage. Then, with a purely ornamental move, the last turn of the dance reveals the souvenir-tattoo etched on her nape like a microchip. A black double-headed eagle, the symbol of Albania's rebelliousness against foreign conquerors.

•

As soon as the show is over, Eliza Dushku gets dressed, says goodnight, and leaves, smacking her gum as forcefully as ever. She comes to work a few more times and then doesn't come back to the shop ever again. I'm finally left alone with my suspicions.

The men.

I've seen the men enter the booths, but I haven't seen them come out when the show is over.

I check the booths. They're all occupied.

I haven't seen any spectators leave because they're all still in there.

They're not exactly corpses, so I don't know if this counts as murder.

The last time, as she was leaving, she said: I left you some good material. She winked at me. I thought she was referring to her striptease-memoir: *Journey Back to the Roots.* She knows I was documenting her, live with my security camera (the camera we found turned on in the underground bunker, the camera that saw everything but didn't see *anything*). I didn't realize she wasn't thinking about coming back.

Why come back, if all the booths are filled to the brim with that white, doughy substance that had been accumulating and piling up ever since her first show. A formless, viscous, pulpy substance in which there was no trace of the men gripping their respective penises. A few cartilaginous lumps here and there, strips of clothing, a red eyeball looking at me from the top layer of the seminal eruption.

When dried, the material has a gumlike quality.

•

There is no gas anywhere, but the mafiosos had a good stash of Havana Club. I open a few bottles. I spray the piles of white trash and throw in a match: They burn marvelously. I sprinkle alcohol all over the shop. The fire blazes. The flames extend like voracious tongues among the videos, magazines, sex toys. I take my things and walk out engulfed in smoke.

Behind me, the shop windows blow.

I start running.

El Grandmaster

I head south, leaving the northern coast behind without looking back. The south is a question without an answer: Where do all those cars come from, and where are they going?

(To Curaçao, Cartagena, Colón, then across the Petrified Panama Canal to continue on to the some of the Galápagos Islands, all covered in cement and gas stations and shopping centers?)

The Venezuelan multimillionaire I run into at the motel has seen it all. He saw the different stages of the supercon-struction, sticking his head out of his private Boeing, fall-ing prey to vertigo. He anchored his most luxurious yacht in the shade of the tallest lanes. There now rose over the Caribbean a zigzagging megastructure, and on it, the drivers defied the day, the night, the ocean winds. Needless to say, this Venezuelan millionaire didn't come by plane or yacht; he took the Freeway.

•

I ask the motel reception if they have a cursed room, the kind nobody would expect a living person to stay in.

"We have a room where a woman killed her husband just a few days ago."

"I'll take it." I pay cash and put a couple of bills in the guy's pocket. "If anybody comes by asking for me (and by 'anybody' I mean anything: a man, woman, extraterrestrial), tell them I'm not here. Okay?"

"There is always going to be someone with more money."

"Thank you." I take the key. "Am I going to find blood-stains or what?"

"The murder? It's a good story."

•

I check out the room.

In the bathroom trash, I find an apple.

There's nothing like a night of good role-play to ignite passion. She dressed as the Prince. He dressed as Snow White, bit into the recently purchased apple, and lay down on the bed. She should have woken him up with a sweet kiss, removed his dress, and raped him. But she didn't do it. The Prince locked the door and took the key. Those who saw her leave in her car thought she was him wearing a ridiculous costume. She peeled out in the middle of the night, tires squealing. The Freeway remixes all of that:

post-toon fantasy, primal desire, the desire to run as far away as possible.

"Hey, you," the apple says to me: the edges of the bite mark move, they become the shape of a mouth. "Do you know who I am? I'm La Manzanita de Apple."

Clearly, the shot of cyanide made her go crazy.

•

I leave the room at dusk. I go to the vending machine. And, for a few minutes, lean against the railing on the first floor, watching the Freeway lights. Watching the motel parking lot.

I watch him arrive.

I watch him get out of the car.

I watch him take a bag out of the Ferrari's trunk. A great big bag.

All of a sudden, he looks up at where I'm standing. I quickly duck into my room. In a short while, I hear noises from the adjacent room. Clicks, vibrations, clangs all night long.

•

"Great! Let's play a game," La Manzanita de Apple says.

The board is ten by ten, it comes with a die and two pieces I've never seen before.

“Why does everything have to be so strange?” I ask myself.

“This is Capablanca Random Chess, which combines the features of Capablanca Chess and of Fischer Random Chess.” La Manzanita de Apple informs me that the two mutant pieces, Capablanca’s innovations, are called “archbishop” (a bishop-knight) and “chancellor” (a rook-knight). The initial placement is random—decided by the roll of the die, as Fischer suggested. The only restrictions are that the bishops should be different colors, the king should be between the rooks, and all the pawns are protected at the beginning. “You can be white, genius. Roll the die.”

Someone knocks on the door.

“Who is it?”

“I hope the noise didn’t bother you,” the voice says.

“What do you want?” I ask.

“Are you alone?”

“Yes.”

“Are you going to stay in there for a while?”

“Depends.”

“You’re going to get bored.”

“I’m already bored.”

“You don’t have to hide from me.”

“Thank you for clearing that up.”

“I’m going to leave you a present out here as a gesture of goodwill. We can talk some other time if you’d like.”

Footsteps fade away.

I wait a while.

I open the door to get the bomb.

On the ground, there is a chessboard. And a note:

"So you can entertain yourself a bit, mi pana. Kasparov gifted it to me. Yes, the very one, Garry Kasparov. I'm from Venezuela—sister nation." (Signed: R. A.)

•

One must keep in mind that the concepts of a new chess variant completely change the general concept of the classic game of chess.

J. R. Capablanca: *Greetings to all. I am here today with a North American colleague I do not know to give you a play-by-play of this game. I should clarify that analysis does not thrill me and that I am not especially interested in theory. I like gentle sports. Tennis, for example. And women's gymnastics.*

Bobby Fischer [swiping at camera]: *Get that away from me. Turn it off. If you don't, I'm leaving right now, and I won't comment about anything. I only want my voice to be heard, like on radio interviews I've done all over the world. For example, on September 11, 2001, in the Philippines. Let the perfectly credible voice of the narrator be heard.*

The initial position determined by the roll of the die (more than random, absurd) forces an improvised opening. I try to follow the standard guidelines: developing the pieces that fight for control of the center. No matter the type of chess, the center is still the center. Is it not?

In order to confuse my opponent, I take a corner pawn and move it three squares forward. La Manzanita de Apple moves the baffling bishop-knight from behind his row of pawns.

BF: *Of course, we had to make modifications. The old chess was dead. Very uncreative. It's all just a bunch of books and memorization. And to make things worse, the Russians, those cunning dogs, would prearrange games among themselves. I saw many things, but above all, I saw the freezing of chess, chess as a kind of cold war. That's why I invented my own rules in order to send textbook positions to hell.*

JRC: *I never studied. My books were the boards, practice, the dresses of European women, training, Russian ballerinas from the 1920s and 1930s . . . At that time, chess was a bit much for my taste—too many boards. The idea was to have a larger board and two new, combined pieces to add splendor to games. But nobody paid any mind—and at the time, I was the most famous Cuban in the world.*

•

His name, the Venezuelan's name, is Roman. Roman Abramovich.

You can find my ELO in *Forbes*, he jokes.

•

I avoid trading pieces in the first moves. First, I should figure out what to do with them on a board that seems huge to me. We soon find ourselves in what is known as a closed position—a place where La Manzanita de Apple appears comfortable.

JRC: *I prefer black. Up to this point, the only thing white has done correctly has been to create weak points.*

BF: *Aren't you being too easy on the white?*

JRC: *It is true that, beyond the board, women can be a certain kind of weakness. And weaknesses can lead you to losing the world title. I am referring to weakness on the board.*

BF: *I don't like American girls. They're very conceited, sabes.*

JRC: *We should side with a language, Bobby. Mientras estemos narrando.*

I now realize castling on this side was not the best decision. I start to worry about the b1-j9 diagonal.

BF: *This girl would send me boxes of chocolates and love letters. She said she was in the crowd watching me play back in Yugoslavia. She said that when I left, the stars fell out of the sky. Turns out, her country was suffering from a sort of embargo. Years later, I remembered those letters, when I wrote to Osama bin Laden to offer my support and tell him that we are both fugitives from the US justice system. I wrote "justice" in quotes.*

•

We drink beer and look at the stars and watch the patrol helicopters fly over the motel. Roman Abramovich tells me about his private army. Four hundred men with a single mission: to protect him. But now, he's alone. The patrol helicopters have nothing to do with him (or with anybody in particular). It was safer to travel incognito, without an entourage of mercenaries. His Enemies probably think he's in Venezuela. The Project should continue to remain in the dark. Tomorrow, he, along with the Project, will continue on their way north, where they'll jump into the Unknown Dimension to draft a Plan.

•

JRC: *After Ce5, what we're looking at is a needlessly complicated position. My suggestion is for both sides to simplify. This is something I've said many times: One must eliminate waffling at the board.*

BF: *I'm glad we're playing this match in a closed room. It reminds me of Iceland in 1972, the match against Spassky for the World Chess Championship. This is what chess is about: It's just you and your opponent at the board, and you're trying to prove something. Kissinger called me and said: "You're our man against the Reds." I couldn't help but remind him that a few years prior, the State Department stopped me from going to the tournament that bears your name, el Memorial Capablanca in La Habana.*

JRC: *I had good friends who were Reds, and, honestly, I thought it was a shame the Reds didn't participate in the 1939 Chess Olympiad in Buenos Aires, where I meant to bid them all farewell. I predicted that Botvinnik would be the world chess champion. Once, in a tournament in Moscow, I noticed Stalin would watch the matches hiding behind a column. I went up to him and said (behind the column): "When the others see a position, they ask themselves what can happen, what will happen; I simply know." Stalin looked at me solemnly. "I can show you," I added. Stalin looked at me more seriously still . . . and now I see that the black pieces are about to destroy the white's structure on the left side.*

That's how it goes. I lose the structure and the pawn. Then, La Manzanita de Apple places her archbishop on f4, and I feel it in the deepest depths of my throat.

•

"I can't take it anymore," Abramovich says. I think he's referring to his beer because he's already pretty drunk. "I can't take it anymore" (he burps), "I have to tell somebody . . . I finally did it, pana. I have recreated Simón Bolívar with parts from different corpses. I have El Libertador in there, in my room. Do you want to see him?"

•

BF: *White won't be able to take the pressure much longer. In Iceland, Spassky couldn't take it either. The Kremlin sent a psychiatrist. I guess one psychologist wasn't enough. But I don't believe in psychiatry, or in psychology. I believe in good moves. All that matters on the chessboard is good moves.*

I'm still worried about the b1-j9 diagonal.

In fact, I'm now worried about all diagonals.

JRC: *The best option is to open the h column and trade pieces. Now the black ones coordinate consolidation.*

BF: *You know, I admire the clarity of your descriptions.*

JRC: *You sound like Olga, my second wife.*

I painstakingly focus on defensive moves, or what I consider to be defensive, maybe they're not. I also don't quite see all the threats, where they are, what they are.

I must proceed with caution and avoid all possible risks. If not, I'll make what they call a blunder. If I don't go mad from playing against a disturbed apple, I may be able to manage a stalemate.

•

On the bed: there is a metal sheet instead of a mattress; on it lies a huge human body, chained by the wrists and ankles, and connected by cables to a series of electric generators. Around his neck, you can see the stitches that join the head and the body; patches and stitches are visible on his face, thick hands, and enormous feet. He's like Frankenstein except he's dressed in a uniform from a history book. His resemblance to Bolívar is unquestionable.

Abramovich stops vomiting and stumbles out of the bathroom.

"What do you think? Now all he needs is a good DC shock."

•

JRC: *I wrote a few things about chess, and Olga would help me with the manuscripts, polishing the parts that were not inherently technical. She would say it rarely needed revision. She would say "something enchanting emanated" from my writing. She praised my ability to write only what was necessary with economy and power. "The way in which you highlight the dynamic elements of the text is exceptional," she would say. "When the rest focus only on the static. You understand like no other the importance of commanding the reader . . ." Olga tried to convince me that I could have been the greatest Cuban writer of the twentieth century. The nonsense Russian women put in your head . . .*

Surprisingly, I fall into a trap, or make a bad move, and I lose a bishop. This means I'm losing, it's only a matter of time. Forget a stalemate.

Perhaps, in this vitamin-enriched chess, a stalemate is impossible. Its design doesn't allow it. The shadows of the diabolical die and the freak dimensions of the pieces lengthen.

I resist a little longer, motivated, above all, by inertia. When I tilt my king to imply surrender, La Manzanita de Apple lifts the corners of her bite-mark mouth: she's smiling. "Checkmate," she says. "That's not checkmate," I say. "I know, but I wanted to say 'checkmate.' It's just that this is my first time . . .and with no hands!"

BF: *The problem is that Spassky, deep down, was a good guy. And the good ones always lose in chess. There are tough chess players and there are good ones. I'm one of the tough ones. Spassky himself defined me as such: "When you play Bobby, it is not a question of whether you win or lose. It is a question of whether you survive." I single-handedly won that match for the United States. And how did they thank me? As soon as they no longer needed me, they launched an international conspiracy against me, headed by Israel. I knew what they were scheming when I read* The Secret World Government, *the book written by the major general of czarist Russia, Arthur Spiridovich. Now that was a well-written book. That is the kind of book writers should write. When I became a target for the* FBI *and* CIA, *I was ready to understand what was behind all that through the secret channels of history.*

•

The dead tissue was electrified and convulsing. The cables sparked. The lights in the room flickered and, all of a sudden, we were left in the dark.

"I think you blew the power of the entire motel," I comment.

"No problem. It's my motel. I bought it. In fact, I bought all the motels between the coasts." Abramovich turns on a floodlight. The light blinds us. When we open our eyes, we see a superstrong Bolívar who has broken the metal chains, removed the electrodes and cables, and is sitting on the bed, putting his boots on.

"He's . . . alive! It's El . . . ! El . . . El . . . Libertador!" Abramovich jumps around, jubilant and nervous. No trace of intoxication.

Simón Bolívar tries taking a few firm steps around the room, he studies his expressionless face in the mirror. He coughs. He beats his chest thunderously and spits out stuffing material. He looks so . . . so calm.

"Can he speak? Can he say . . . anything?" I ask Roman in a low voice, but he doesn't answer, he doesn't see me. I decide to leave discreetly, closing the door without making a sound. I didn't get to finish listening to his welcoming speech:

"Oh, general! Oh, master! You cannot possibly imagine how much I have (. . .)"

•

BF: *Looks like the white pieces conceded. That's the best thing they could have done.*

JRC: *There were times in my life in which I was very close to believing I could not lose a single match. I thought I was undefeatable. But then it turned out that I was in fact not undefeatable, and defeat forced me to get grounded.*

BF: *There were times in my life I would throw pieces up in the air and they would land in the correct squares. In that stupid game we just watched, the white pieces fell over and over again onto the wrong squares.*

JRC: *Nothing is healthier than a good beating at just the right moment. I didn't learn as much from the games I won as I did from my defeats. It is true I had few defeats, so I didn't have many opportunities to learn.*

BF: *Well, our game is over . . . Shall we review the highlights?*

JRC: *Can we just stop talking about chess and remain silent forever?*

[. . .]

BF: *Tell me, which one was the best? What would we relive?*

JRC: *Saint Petersburg, 1914: the Czar (the last Czar) awarded me the title of Grandmaster.*

BF: *Renouncing the title of world chess champion immediately after receiving it. I would do it again.*

JRC: *Never, under any circumstance, live or act like a* GM *only because a czar has awarded you the title of* GM.

BF: *Walking on the face of the earth like a celebrity, like a playboy, like a visionary, like a monster nobody understands.*

JRC: *The first time I defeated the great Lasker in the*

United States, he told me: "Son, you don't make mistakes." And I thought: Why would I make any mistakes?

BF: *Renouncing US citizenship and becoming an Icelandic citizen. At the end of the day, I, too, put an island on the map. Just like you did.*

JRC: *The Cuban embassy in the United States, the best place in the world to be an economic adviser (perhaps, deep down, it's what I've always been).*

BF: *Japanese prison, where I realized I could have been a different person if the world hadn't changed me.*

JRC: *The Manhattan Chess Club.*

BF: *The Manhattan Chess Club, of course. And the instant your opponent writhes before you. The sound a man's ego makes when it shatters into pieces.*

JRC: *We could go on like this all night, Bobby . . .*

•

At daybreak, standing against the railing, I watch them leave. The Venezuelan multimillionaire and his companion (who can't drive) go who-knows-where and for-who-knows-how-long.

The Ferrari's tires kick up dust in the parking lot.

Las Girls Gone Wild

And there it was, the first accident on the Freeway. A fire blazing. A tanker truck flipped in the air. It must have been a spectacular sight.

El Autista could see the smoke from the desert.

•

"What is that?" he asks.

Behind the motel, there's some sort of industrial or military polygon. It looks like they never started, or never finished, building something. In the middle, we find a deep pit.

"It was probably going to be a pool," I tell him.

"If it were filled with water, I'd jump in right now and stay underwater forever," El Autista's car says. "Either way, I've already sunk."

Now El Autista calls him "El Autismóvil." He looks at himself in the rearview mirror and adjusts his mask. Then he looks at the camera, expressionless.

"I thought they had killed you," I say by way of greeting.

He tells me what happened. There isn't the slightest guarantee his story is true, but here it goes anyway. That's all we've got.

"We have company," El Autismóvil warns.

We look around.

Nobody.

The empty pit. Stacked bricks. A few beams. Boxes. Broken drums. Aridity.

But El Autismóvil feels the ground tremble.

"A stampede approaches."

•

Even though they don't look like it, they're girls. Females. Confirmed by voices and poses and gestures they can't control. Young, in their teens, all very skinny: flat chests, flat asses, no hips. Some have shaved their heads.

They roll in on fabulous skateboards.

They scream:

"A ramp!!!"

They take turns on the ramp-pit.

One of them waves her tattooed arms, trying to get my attention:

"Hey, cameraman! Wanna film something fun?"

•

El Autista talks about the desert landscape as if it were an elaborate chart with its own flows and figures. Killing someone out here is nothing more than an abstract gesture. One's heroism is supported by the contours of a dune.

What happened:

The mafiosos put him in the truck. The mafiosos took him out of the car at gunpoint. They told him he had taken his *abilities* too seriously. They joked back and forth. Laughing, they aimed at him. All of a sudden, one of them shifted his attention and his gun. ¿Qué cojones es eso? he asked, pointing at the floor. A strange animal watching from the sand. One of those mixed species that abound in the desert. Bulging eyes, hooked beak, a pair of wings with black feathers, and long hind legs with webbed feet. Too big to be a frog or toad, too small to be part of the vulture family. El Autista classified him a "buitracio."

"A biological weapon?" one of the mafiosos suggested. The other one focused on shooting the creature.

The bullet hit a rock instead. It ricocheted and hit another rock, and after hitting the third rock, of course, it reached somebody it wasn't aimed at.

"Ahhh . . . me cago en tu madre," the wounded man said. Before dying, he shot the other one (who was still in shock) in the head.

Two shots. The buitracio, or whatever it was, suddenly flew away. El Autista was the only one by the dead bodies.

•

The skater chicks turn out to be very good. From one end of the ramp-pit, they come and go doing their stunts, their tricks. Aerial techniques that would sweep the X Games. They bare all for the camera. Even their tears.

They say:

"If we did it once, we can do it again."

They say:

"It's always a challenge, there's nothing routine about any roll. And we're all crazy, which just accentuates our beauty."

They say:

"You forget everything else. Deep down, you're just trying to free yourself from your body."

They say:

"You're going to be the judges because you're men."

They've quickly put together a beauty pageant: Miss Skate. Faded and ripped shirts, thick belts, knee pads, and other accessories that look big and unattractive. All set. Places, everyone.

Let's check this out.

•

El Autista talks about crossing the desert as a mechanism of adaptation. A way of breathing, walking, thinking . . .

He walked for hours.

He saw cow skeletons. Whole skeletons of deer laying out in the sun.

He saw strange burrows hidden in the marabú trees.

He saw, in the distance, a pillar of smoke. He had to choose a path and decided to follow it. It was the return to the Freeway.

He found broken barricades. He found an overturned truck on the edge of a slope. The driver had managed to crawl out before the cabin exploded. When El Autista arrived, he was already on his feet.

"Look at that, bro, I'm soaked," he moaned. The guy had just been in a wreck but was doing impressive flips around big puddles. El Autista read the contents of the truck: LIQUID ADRENALINE. A truck full of adrenaline had literally fallen on him.

Adrenaline Rush, thought El Autista.

"I'm covered in oil," the truck driver said.

"No, it's not oil, it's . . ."

"It's a curse. An irony. To come here to die, covered in oil, many years after the Oil Rush."

"Mi socio, you're delirious." Post-traumatic stress, El Autista thought. "Why don't you lie down for a bit."

But El Post-Traumático didn't even sit down. He just started walking away from the Freeway. Accustomed to following a trace (of industrial liquids, of bloody entrails), El Autista followed him.

It was the return to the desert.

•

LaLonelyGirl09/

Sign: Aquarius. Color: frosty pink. Blood type: A-negative. Punctuation mark: parenthesis. Status: available. 75,204 falls. Favorite quote: "I don't think anyone approaches me for intellectual conversation" (Megan Fox).

LaRedCow/

Looks like Ashton Kutcher, though much younger and two hundred pounds lighter. "I'm a little anorexic, a little bulimic, I'm not totally fine, but I don't think any of us are." Her skateboard says: GOODBYE REDBULL.

•

El Post-Traumático walked with remarkable speed despite having two broken legs, a bone splinter poking through his skin, a cracked-open skull, a strip of metal across his ribs, and shards of glass all over his body.

And he wouldn't stop talking.

"I'd like to be remembered as a veteran. A Gulf Vet. The Gulf of México. We came to these shores to find black gold..."

El Autista was curious. He asked himself how far El Post-Traumático could continue in this condition. How long would his delirium last?

"No, nobody came," he said. "There was never any gold of any color."

"Yes, I was here. Right here. I saw it all, years ago . . ."

With tears welling in his eyes, El Post-Traumático looked at the landscape-mirage that silently extended before him. There, where El Autista had seen only death and marabous, El Post-Traumático saw mines, wells, towns, and bars.

•

LaMoxxxilla/

They tell us they come from different places, different devasted towns. They have come together along the way. Exploring. They take over the ruins they find, they modify the landscape and *roll* with it. They can rest anywhere, or they don't rest at all and keep practicing and keep moving. They're drifters. They have nothing. "But skating keeps us going."

LaFlyingPapaya/

Sign: Pisces. Color: dazzling yellow. Shampoo: dry hair. Mammal: manatee. Current: constant. 95,873 fractures. Favorite quote: "I wish God were alive to see this" (Homer Simpson).

LaSkinnyBitch/

Shows her lower-body tattoos: pinup girls, small ink dolls that coil around her long legs. She's worried about the relay. "I'd like to tell girls that it's okay to be sexy, and that we shouldn't be afraid of skateboards."

•

According to El Post-Traumático, if we're to believe El Autista, the most improbable news scattered like gunpowder. Oil in Cuba . . . and so much of it! The Island, a great platform. El Post-Traumático was one of the first to enlist. They came in planes and aircraft carriers. It was the beginning of what was later called the Oil Rush.

"Many arrived anxious and scared to death. They had heard all kinds of stories about the violence in the region. But I wasn't afraid of the Wild South. I'm Hispanic, bro. I was born in Puerto Rico."

"La isla de la libertad," as Marc Anthony's salsa song goes, was idealized by El Post-Traumático's parents. They fled when he was a boy, and the boy grew up hearing, frequently and nostalgically, about Puerto Riquísimo.

"But when I arrived, I realized Cuba was not what I expected. Chaos reigned. The military and the civilian blurred together. There was no private property, contracts, taxes. There was no real government in place. It was a lawless territory. A territory, a *frontier*, as it was called at the time."

El Autista imagined bubbles. A great thought bubble over El Post-Traumático illustrated the scenery that was ready to be transformed into a great bubble of riches. And the bubbles (even thought bubbles) don't blow up with norms and regulations, but with the absence of these.

•

LaDulciiisima/

Redhead, freckles, a specimen of the Viking genotype. She blows bubbles with her chewing gum that leave bits on her nose when they pop. There is something unsettling and wicked about her face.

LaSk8erBitch/

Sign: Scorpio. Color: superwhite. Sign: No Parking. Passport: fake. Symptoms: nervous. 48,204 scars. Favorite quote: "Blondes are like virgin snow that shows up the bloody footprints" (Alfred Hitchcock).

•

Wells perforated the entire landscape. If you stabbed a pin into the ground, oil would squirt out. That's just how it was.

And in each drilling zone, there was at least one Saloon. They propagated in parallel: on the one side, towers and pipes and pumps, and on the other, the locals decompressing from work.

Ah, the old Saloons . . . El Post-Traumático said. The peaceful moments in the midst of the underground battle. Saloons for drinking whiskey. For playing poker and listening to folk music. Saloons for imagining business deals. For ruminating on projects. For contemplating the most profound mysteries of oil, the millennial rocks, generators of crude (the product of the decomposition of marine organisms), the need for fuel to search for more fuel.

Ah, the Saloon and the girls . . . El Post-Traumático heaved. Cameras. Dancers. Beautiful legs and resounding nicknames: Miss Rebeca, Miss Laura, Miss Annabel . . . you could take any of them to bed for just a few dollars. What happened to the girls, bro? Where are they? What happened to their unbreakable bodies and their great feelings of love? In the toughest of times, they made the Wild South seem worth it.

Because it wasn't easy, claro. The death toll continued to rise. The living didn't miss out on a single opportunity. Disputes over control of the oilfields were resolved with shootouts. Bullets zipped by all the time. The empty, dusty streets witnessed cinematographic duels. Beyond the illusion, it all boiled down to this: constant danger, perpetual guerrilla.

The guerrilla.

The natives. Of course. Maybe they weren't the greatest island civilization to have ever existed, but they also weren't about to hand over their lands, their resources, and their traditions without causing any problems.

•

LaSuperMerMaid/

Thinking about retiring, popping her last ollie on this

ramp and doing something else. Feels a change is necessary (especially a change in topic). She's very young and needs to have experiences. "Who knows? Maybe I'll find a boyfriend, or a pet, or get pregnant again."

LaDarkpassenger/

Sign: Gemini. Color: pearl gray. Particle: neutrino. Breakfast: hard-boiled eggs. Allergies: pollen, plankton. 39,611 dislocations. Favorite quote: "If I had a heart, it would be breaking right now" (Dexter Morgan).

LaKittyKatty/

Tells us about the learning process, consciousness-raising, and control. Tames the skateboard, tames herself, becomes a beautiful tamed animal. "Form and content begin to emerge, and these begin to take control little by little." (*Control* seems to be the operative word.)

•

El Post-Traumático was now showing signs of exhaustion. He limped. El Autista held him up by the waist to help him conserve energy. It felt as if everything inside this guy was loose. But, if he could keep going, he should keep going.

And El Post-Traumático kept telling him about the guerrilla. Many stories have been told, he said, most were exaggerated. You know how that is. The newspapers would say: If the facts don't align with the legend, print the legend.

He saw the facts with his own eyes. No epic to be found.

A group of natives captured him during a confrontation. He thought they were going to kill him. He said his goodbyes to his loved ones, especially to his parents. All of a sudden, memories invaded him. He returned to his childhood, to his parents, to the raft in the middle of the sea, to the death that was rocking him in the form of black waves.

The raft was a precarious artifact made from tires and wooden boards. He sailed aboard it with Papá and Mamá, along the coast of Puerto Riquísimo. Thousands set out to sea in similar conditions. They were known as "balseros." The goal was to reach New York. At the end of the day, the distance was a little more than twenty-five hundred miles.

He watched Arecibo, his hometown, disappear over the horizon. Leaving behind what had been his life up to that point. Leaving behind the enormous dish-shaped telescope that inspired many dreams: the radio telescope at the Arecibo Observatory, where his father used to work. Even though he was only an operator, his father would tell him all about the marvels of space. He would say, for example, that life existed on other planets—we just had to look for it. The radio telescope did just that: detected signals that might reveal extraterrestrial life. Our radio telescope is an invaluable resource for exobiologists, his father said proudly. What are exobiologists, Papá? The ones who study extraterrestrial life, hijo. And the son declared he would become an exobiologist when he grew up. His father told him nothing would get in the way of him realizing his dreams once he was in New York.

Although he didn't know it, El Pre-Post-Traumático would never realize any of his dreams, not even his future dream of striking oil.

They slowly crossed the wide and desolate Sargasso Sea, where the currents were weak, where it didn't rain much, and where the water was terribly salty. An inhospitable region for marine organisms and rafting organisms (except for the sargassum and a few eels, the Sargasso Sea was a great biological desert). As if that weren't enough, more than half of the voyage consisted of crossing the Bermuda Triangle from one end to the other, also known as the Devil's Triangle. If ships and even airplanes would get lost and disappear in that condemned ecosystem, what would you expect for a rudimentary raft? Thousands of rafters vanished, they disintegrated, they evaporated there. This did not deter the other thousands of hopeful NY-bound rafters.

Despite all this, there were castaways from Puerto Riquísimo that did arrive unharmed from the Desert and the Triangle, and, after months of drifting, got to see the Statue of Liberty. El Post-Traumático was one of the lucky ones who made it to Manhattan. Years later, he would thoroughly understand the extent of his luck. Years later, he would be captured alive by the natives on an island bigger than his own and think: There is no way I'll make it through this one.

Against all odds, the natives didn't kill him.

•

LaButterflyDefect/

She has an I♥NYBISH T-shirt. Who is Nybish? Nobody. We wish. (I♥NY But I'm Still Here.)

LaBestialittle/

Wears a small shell around her neck. A miniature conch. Her amulet. She says that if she blows it like a whistle (she blows it), it produces an inaudible sound that summons native demons.

LaPussyPower7/

She says she can't express herself verbally very well. "I don't want to sound cynical." There's nothing else to say. She doesn't keep indefinable secrets. She doesn't chase unattainable dreams. She's not a raped Cinderella and isn't wearing armor. "This is what I do. This is what there is. That's it."

LaLolitoon/

Sign: Virgo. Color: mauve. Treatment: antibiotics. Dessert: ice cream. Ice cream: strawberry chocolate chip. 62,967 X-rays. Favorite quote: "The basic clay of our work is the youth" (Ernesto Guevarra).

•

The adrenaline evaporated in the sun. El Post-Traumático could no longer walk.

He now dragged himself in the sand.

It looked like he wanted to go somewhere. But there was nowhere to go.

He said they kept him captive in a remote village. Maybe they kept him to trade prisoners. The trade never happened. With time, the natives lost all interest in him. He could have easily escaped. He assessed the situation. His opportunities were the only things escaping. If he couldn't get rich in the midst of the Oil Rush, it was never going to happen. The last thing he wanted was to go back north the same way he left and get stuck in a miserable job. Route trucker, for example.

No. Everything he had been through was going to serve him somehow. He didn't have any natural resources; he was going to take advantage of his only stock: his experiences.

Write a book.

My Life with the Wild Natives. Bestseller.

Opening line: "If you're into indigenismo, underdevelopment, or shit like that, honestly, I recommend you stop reading now."

Little by little, El Post-Traumático earned his captors' trust, he learned their language, he socialized. At night, he would sit around the fire. He listened attentively. He discovered the stories of the natives were an inexhaustible well. A well of underground tradition. His book project took an unexpected turn. He quickly took notes in a notebook for a potential study.

•

Features that would be present in this Cuban narrative:

a) Blurred Genres: The lines that separate genres are not well defined, so that a narrative may appear to belong neither to a single genre nor to any combination of genres.

b) Weak Narrative Unity: Long narratives are not sustained thematically nor by the presentation of an argument (which is usually inconsistent and absurd), but by the drifting of a character through a sequence of connected experiences.

c) Fluidity of Content: Each event is detached from the previous. The stories are, basically, aggregations and collections.

d) Animal/Human/Machine Ambiguity: The most evident and clearest characteristic of all. Self-explanatory.

e) Surrealist Space-Time: The events cannot be placed within a realistic timeline or chronological frame. They occur in different dimensions (but which ones?). Nevertheless, it can be empirically demonstrated that these cause *curvatures* in what is real.

f) Carbonated Style: Being a narrative that is orally transmitted, it's associated with bodily gases, with respiration, with the current atmospheric humidity, and, above all, with the smoke of the war pipe. Its oral quality places it outside the worldwide publishing market. (To put it in writing will also not do much. This kind of style will never be lucrative.)

•

The time for the final judgment has arrived. We have seen all the girls in action. Possessed. Self-powered. We have closely examined their androgyny, their physical effort pushed to the edge, their monstrosity . . .

It's clear we're never going to agree, El Autista and I. It's clear we don't have the slightest understanding of the technical elements that would determine the winner.

"We can choose the winner at random," El Autista proposes. "By throwing a skateboard up in the air."

"In case you need to break a tie, you know, a third vote . . ." El Autismóvil says. "Don't count on me."

"I thought you were jotting down your impressions of each one here," I say as I leaf through my former DB notebook. El Autista has appropriated it. He's already filled out all of his notebooks (there are thousands) with who knows what.

"Impressions?" he says. "What impressions?"

We finally agree to crown the one who reaches the highest air.

In a vertical sense.

•

He couldn't go on like this. He was a corpse who had exhausted all his energy. He sweated his last drop of Oil

Rush Fever and the hallucination abandoned him right at the end.

"Where am I?" he asked himself, looking around. "In the damn desert . . . Now I understand . . . That's why I'm so fucked . . . My body hurts, it's heavy . . ."

El Autista squatted next to him to hold his hand.

"Are you also . . . ?" El Post-Traumático asked him.

"No, bro. Sorry. I'm okay."

"What are you, a damn superhero?"

His famous last words.

When he finished burying El Post-Post-Traumático (very close to the two mafiosos), El Autista contemplated the horizon. He saw another pillar of smoke coming from the Freeway. Another accident, he thought. My work is never done.

And he went over there and found the scorched remains of the sex shop. La Gusanera had burned down. He rummaged through the merchandise that was still intact and found a mask. A velvet one. He put it on. In the parking lot, El Autismóvil was waiting for him, covered in soot.

El Autista sat at the wheel.

"Go," he ordered.

"If you insist," the car said and started the engine.

It was a post-fuel vehicle. It's not like it had been in an accident or anything; it was a car that belonged to a rugged species. It used its tires like little legs. When it took off, its entire body moved in a wavelike motion. For a few moments, it arched and writhed like a mechanical caterpillar.

In general, though, one might say it *crept* as if it were an alloy made from different types of reptiles.

And just like that, slowly, very slowly, step by step, parallel to the Freeway, from parking lot to parking lot, from ditch to ditch, bypassing fences, they finally reached the motel.

•

El Autista on camera:

". . . and when I arrived at the motel, I knocked on a random door and it turned out to be the door to a parallel universe. In that parallel universe, in that parallel motel room, we were there, you and I (I saw myself, and I opened the door . . . or it could have been you, I don't know) were engrossed in a T-shirt printing business. We had turned the motel room into a secret post-production lab. We had discovered a way of printing the documentary onto T-shirts. Something like YouTube T-shirts. We sold them there, as Freeway souvenirs (you and I thought a customer had come to the door . . . in other words, me). That was probably the only way to get people to watch the documentary. These same customers would then project, promote, and distribute it. I suspect we were making a lot of money from the product. I would have bought one or two, but I didn't have any money."

•

And the winner is . . .

La Flying Papaya. She's so happy. Look at her. She can't believe it. Applause. Applause. They all hug and kiss the snazzy Miss Skate. What are you feeling? Still recovering from the shock, she stutters "It's . . . it's the happiest day of my life . . . but . . . but I know that today it's my turn to be on top and on the cover of all the magazines, and tomorrow it'll be somebody else . . . tha . . . that's how these things go, right? I'd like to dedicate this victory to . . ."

They inspire Miss Skate to debut her crown in an exclusive show. Covered in silk ribbons and bows, euphoric, La Flying Papaya jumps on her skateboard and then descends the ramp:

Somersaults.

Turns.

She goes up.

She goes up very high.

All of a sudden something goes wrong up there. The grip. The skateboard goes in one direction and Miss Skate in the other. The girls cover their faces, they cover their mouths, their eyes . . .

La Flying Papaya falls from a great height. Headfirst.

A spectacular dive.

The helmet hits the bottom of the pit. The impact is so great that the ground cracks, and water squirts out. Miss Skate doesn't get up: the stream is strong, and the water surrounds her. The water—which has little black, oily ribbons and probably comes from a forgotten well, or a tank, or, without going too far, from the phreatic layer—begins to fill the pit. The girls are now paralyzed, muted.

Then they yell:

"A pool!"

They quickly take off their clothes, their tennis shoes, their accessories. There they are, very naked in the scrawny splendor and general absence of secondary sex characteristics of their flesh.

They yell:

"Biiikiiiiiniiiiiiis!!!"

And they run like a pack toward the viewer. The image turns, it spins. They have knocked the camera down. The still image captures the rear side of the motel. The shot is unbearably long. You can hear in the background the cameraman shrieking.

Me.

They bite my skin off. They rip my skin off with their hands. I'm not sure where their nails came from. Before fading away, I realize my skin is going to be (it already is, it always has been) the fabric of their bikinis. They skin me, fighting among themselves for the best swatches. In the midst of the greatest pain I've ever felt, I manage to see one (which one?), filthy and drooling, trying on a bloody triangle of my skin over her nipple. Then everything fades to black.

•

LaVictoria'sSecretAngel/

Sign: Cancer. Color: gold. Fruit: forbidden. Record: secret. Donor: endocrine glands. Pressure: omotic. Genre: terror. 1,754,296 blood transfusions. Favorite quote: "Those who have only read about me don't get me" (Paris Hilton).

El Horror

I remember:

Darkness shrouds everything. Darkness, like a strait-jacket, constrains me. The pressure, dull and constant, moving slowly over every nerve ending. A threshold that holds an avalanche of pain. I desperately try to move away from it without moving my body, trying to keep the cries in my mind from escaping.

That's all.

The feeling of isolation.

If anything, a sound, far, far away. Like a negative number of revving engines on a phantom freeway.

•

El Autista stopped at a gas station. I need help, he said. There were two men. The men thought the problem was with El Autismóvil. With its strange way of walking by using tires as if they weren't wheels, as if the most important invention in the world was somehow shameful now. I need help, El Autista calmly repeated. The men recommended a shop a few kilometers ahead. The best mechanic in these parts.

El Autista left.

(He was wearing a mask, one of the men said a while later. Then added: And I believe there was a blistering mannequin in the backseat. The other man nodded, he looked up at the clouds, he took a long drag from his cigarette. We did the right thing, he said.)

In El Autismóvil's back seat, there was a skinned bulge, a bloody, unconscious mass.

Me.

•

I open my eyes. I don't know where I am. I see a roof and dirty walls. I get out of a bed that squeaks horribly. The bed is in the corner of a small room filled with a bunch of junk. Flashbacks flood my mind.

I pat my face and examine my body.

Yes.

I have skin.

I have grown new skin.

•

There was nobody in the shop. Carrying my body on his back, El Autista walked down a hallway and opened the door at the end. A room with a bed, nicely made. Somebody's bedroom. He opened the door on the side. A bathroom. He opened the other door. A paper bag full of junk, oil, dust, and a mat that was clearly unoccupied. He left me there. He thought there was nothing else he could do. He thought I was in a sort of coma and that maybe it would be best if I never woke up.

•

I exit the room. A hallway. I don't see anybody. Next to the room, there's a bathroom. I put on a pair of coveralls that I find in the hamper. Then, suddenly, there, in the mirror over the sink . . . *I see myself.*

It's me, but it's not me. My face is no longer my face.

The skin that has grown back isn't exactly my old skin. I guess this wouldn't be a problem if it weren't for the skin on my face.

I have El Autista's face now.

I close my eyes and think: If I'm still asleep, this would be a good time to wake up.

•

El Autista was leaving when the shop owner appeared.

"Interesting vehicle you have out there," he commented. "I almost bumped into it, and then it said a bunch of things to me I'd rather not repeat."

He was small, dressed in coveralls, and wore sunglasses.

The sunglasses covered much more than his eyes; they covered a third of his face.

"Ban," he introduced himself. "Ray Ban," and he extended his hand out to El Autista. And with that, El Autista realized the small man was blind.

•

I walk out of the bathroom and run into him. We look at each other. It's the same face I just examined in the bathroom. Except he's wearing a mask around his eyes that makes them stand out and imbues them with mystery—even if it's a mystery we both know is impractical. El Autista doesn't look surprised, he doesn't say anything about my new Autista look. It seems as if he's never looked at himself or as if he has already forgotten what we used to be.

"How much time has passed?" I ask.

"Since when?" he asks me.

•

Blind and all, Ray Ban repairs all kinds of cars with maximum efficiency. He explained to El Autista that the senses of the blind develop to unforeseeable limits. He can simply listen to the engine's sound, or touch a cable, or inhale the air from an open hood, and, with that, diagnose the problem. The cars, he was sure, *spoke* to him. Then, his hands moved as if each tool knew exactly what to do on its own.

"These supersenses are like superpowers, right?" Ray Ban told El Autista, smiling indiscreetly.

He added:

"For example, I don't need to be able to see you to know you're covering your face. I don't need to be able to see what you look like to know you're wearing a mask."

•

"Vaya, you finally removed that thing from your face," Ray Ban says, directed at me.

I whisper into El Autista's ear:

"Is this the blind man?"

"Don't worry, your secret is safe with me," Ray Ban says. "I can't see you, so I don't know who you are."

"I'm somebody else," I tell him. "I'm not the one you think you're talking to."

"Of course not." Ray Ban turns suddenly to El Autista. "You put the mask on again! You think I wouldn't notice?"

"Hey, there's two of us," El Autista says and gestures: "One, two."

"Yeah, yeah. Double identity, secret identity. Yes, I know all about that."

El Autista takes me aside, to the corner of the shop, and recaps:

"I think he perceives us as one person."

•

Despite his special powers, Ray Ban didn't consider himself a mechanic, but rather, a critic. A critic of what? El Autista asked him. Film, art, literature, all of that, Ray Ban responded. He had been one of the most important critics on the Island, and now might be only one. The last one. I am alone. I have been left behind, Ray Ban said. And so, I have a great responsibility.

•

"One last drink," Ray Ban proposes. He opens up a Havana Club and fills two empty oil cans. He hands me one. "Since you removed your mask, I suppose your work, your mission here, is over. Am I wrong?"

I indulge him:

"No, you're not wrong."

"So . . . are you leaving?"

"Tomorrow," El Autista says, distracted. "I'm tired . . . You might ask: *Tired of what*?"

"Tomorrow," I repeat.

Ray Ban listens only to me and nods. His sunglasses obscure an expression of infinite serenity.

•

Even though, at the moment, he was only considered to be a mechanic, all that was about to change. Ray Ban regularly frequented local establishments: the warehouses, bars, kiosks, tents, other shops . . . The endless fringes on both sides of the Freeway—wherever drivers might stop for a coffee, to pee, spit, wash windshields, or stretch their legs, Ray Ban had bombarded the place with copies and copies of this promotional flyer:

EL CRITIC

DO YOU KNOW WHERE YOU ARE STANDING?
DO YOU KNOW WHAT IS UNDERNEATH THE FREEWAY?
DO YOU KNOW "THE ROOTS?"

WHICH BOOKS OR MAGAZINES OR DVDS OR OLD POSTCARDS WOULD YOU BUY IN THE HYPOTHETICAL CASE THAT BOOKS OR MAGAZINES OR DVDS OR OLD POSTCARDS WERE SOLD AT SOME DAMNED KILOMETER BETWEEN KEY WEST AND CAYO LARGO?

LISTEN TO AN EXPERT

ANALYSIS COMMENTARY REVIEWS

$5 ONLY

•

Ray Ban knew his role and mission well: His was the struggle to restore memory and knowledge against speed and the elements. Because nothing had yet been lost, even though everything seemed hopelessly lost. Because what had to be restored and salvaged was nothing more or less than the fundamental core of la cultura cubana.

•

A Nissan stops at the shop entrance. Ray Ban goes out to meet it holding a small can of oil.

"Something's not right," the driver explains. "Would you mind taking a look?"

"I'm all done for today," the blind man says.

"But . . ."

"I'm sorry. It's getting dark."

•

Customers kept coming, one after the next, without having come across any copies of *El Critic.* Their needs were less spiritual. That didn't stop Ray Ban. While he worked, lying underneath bodies or leaning over an engine, he would fire up a long monologue—for free—for the stranded driver.

The deep monologue of la cultura cubana.

It was strange listening to him, El Autista told me.

After a certain point, customers would faint from listening. One after the next, they would all collapse. Ray Ban would then take the unconscious bodies to a room in the back of the shop. He would place them down on an old mat and leave them there, one or two or three days, until they recovered. They *always* recovered.

"I'm glad to hear it," El Autista said.

"Why don't you stay tonight?" Ray Ban proposed. "It's getting late . . . and the mat is free."

El Autista had good reason to doubt that. Ray Ban insisted:

"I have never said this to anybody, but for a long while . . . let's see if you can understand . . . the thing is that . . . I . . . I'm terribly afraid of the dark."

There are no light bulbs or lamps in the shop—nothing that emits light. A blind man has no need for such things.

El Autista stood in the door of Ray Ban's room not knowing what to do, avoiding looking at the other door, the one to the room with the comatose bodies.

Ray Ban stumbled onto his bed. Through a small window, the sky, speckled with flashes from the Freeway, consumed the last rays of sunlight.

"What are your superpowers?" he asked, his voice choked.

"I don't have any," El Autista said.

And then the darkness accelerated.

•

The next day in the shop, El Autista found a portable television that only played static. He connected the camera to it, rewound the tape . . . and opaque colors filled the screen. El Autista turned the volume up. He never thought that this moment would be possible. What is this? Ray Ban interrupted him. The documentary about the Freeway we were making, El Autista responded. You and who else? Ray Ban asked.

•

I turn off the television.

Finally.

I don't know what to say.

"And what did he say?"

"He fell asleep," El Autista tells me.

Ray Ban tightens screws and talks to himself. The other person, the driver of an Audi, has earplugs. The plugs were fashioned just in time from a piece of paper. *El Critic.*

"The next night was no less terrifying," El Autista continues.

•

Every day, after sunset, Ray Ban would end his mechanicritic work and then go off to bed. At nightfall, he would sink into the sheets, he would sink into fear. He would place the pillow over his head and would tremble with fear. He would fall asleep, but that didn't make the fear go away. Just the opposite. It was amplified in awful nightmares. Ray Ban would moan like a child, his screams sounded like great howls of pain. Every morning he would wake up in a dense, cold sweat.

Ray Ban sat in front of the television and listened intently to the documentary. El Autista offered to narrate the images. Every so often, El Critic would nod approvingly and offer sound judgment.

He would say:

"Shocking."

He would say:

"Visionary."

He would say:

"There's much to talk about."

But he never reached the end. El Autista caught him with his neck completely pressed against the back of the armchair. Sound asleep.

He played the documentary again the next day. The images were the same, but El Autista changed his narration. Ray Ban fell asleep again.

He played it again the following day. El Autista described images that did not come up on the screen, images that could not have been recorded anywhere, images of a director's cut that cut just about everything.

And once again. Ray Ban ended up snoring. He never reached the end of the documentary. An end, on the other hand, that would be impossible to reach.

The documentary was (and is) inconclusive.

•

Ray Ban is a bulge on the bed. I can barely see him. The dark room is already too dark. But I hear him: He wails and twists and says No! No! No! At times it seems like he's drowning . . .

I don't know what El Autista was doing, every single night, sitting here, the mask keeping his eyes wide open, while my skin was growing back next door. Now he's the one sleeping on that old mat while I keep watch. A watchman without anything concrete to watch for. Because, what else could possibly trigger such an extreme panic attack? Where does it creep in? What could possibly be out there, in there, in the dark of the night, that brings Ray Ban to such a state? Infernal shadows? Open, drooling jaws? Flying octopuses with incredibly long tentacles? The guardian of la memoria cubana morphs into a hopeless man with broken nerves. Such a thing could be attributed to Absolute Evil. The kind that drags you to the brink of insanity over and over again and against which nobody can protect you.

I don't know what I'm doing here.

Acting as the only witness of whatever is happening here.

That's all.

•

He was asleep. El Autista approached him and took off his sunglasses.

Underneath his sunglasses, another pair of identical sunglasses. El Autista removed those, too. Underneath a third set appeared, a fourth, and so on. Sunglasses, one over another, each covering the next. El Autista never reached his eyes.

•

We left the shop in the morning. A few hours later, El Autista and I parted ways.

"Are you sure?" I ask him.

"Yes, I'm staying."

"What are you going to do? There's nothing here."

"You're wrong. Everything is here."

"Only for you, Autista." I smile.

"I'm going to cry," El Autismóvil says.

I watch him fade into the desert in his paraplegic, talking car. The Freeway awaits. Freewheeling.

The first car to stop.

Going north or south?

•

I reach out my hand. I raise my thumb.

I know somebody will understand.

Acknowledgments

Freeway: La Movie includes quotes from the following sources:

Arendt, Christopher and Lily Percy. "What It Feels Like . . . to Be a Prison Guard at Guantánamo Bay." *Esquire,* August 2008.

Carlson, Peter. *Roughneck: The Life and Times of Big Bill Haywood.* New York: W. W. Norton and Company, 1983.

Love, Courtney. *Dirty Blonde: The Diaries of Courtney Love.* London: Faber and Faber, 2006

Jorge Enrique Lage is a Cuban novelist and short-story writer. He is also the editor of the magazine *El cuentero* and the publishing house Caja China of the Onelio Jorge Cardoso Literary Training Center. Formerly a biochemist at the University of Havana, he quit the biosciences right after graduating with honors to pursue a career as a writer. His stories have appeared in anthologies and magazines in Cuba and abroad. His story "Bitches" was published in *McSweeney's 46: Thirteen Crime Stories from Latin America,* and his story "Epilogue with Superhero and Fidel" appeared in the anthology *Cuba in Splinters: Eleven Stories from the New Cuba*(OR Books, 2014).

Lourdes Molina teaches Spanish language and Spanish and Spanish American literature at Southern Methodist University in Dallas. She received her PhD in twentieth-century Latin American literature and history from the University of Texas at Dallas, focusing on Cuban studies and literary translation.

PARTNERS

FIRST EDITION MEMBERSHIP
Anonymous (9)
Donna Wilhelm

TRANSLATOR'S CIRCLE
Ben & Sharon Fountain
Meriwether Evans
Perdrix Ventures

PRINTER'S PRESS MEMBERSHIP
Allred Capital Management
Robert Appel
Charles Dee Mitchell
Cullen Schaar
David Tomlinson & Kathryn Berry
Jeff Leuschel
Judy Pollock
Loretta Siciliano
Lori Feathers
Mary Ann Thompson-Frenk & Joshua Frenk
Matthew Rittmayer
Nick Storch
Pixel and Texel
Social Venture Partners Dallas
Stephen Bullock

AUTHOR'S LEAGUE
Christie Tull
Farley Houston
Jacob Seifring
Lissa Dunlay
Stephen Bullock
Steven Kornajcik
Thomas DiPiero

PUBLISHER'S LEAGUE
Adam Rekerdres
Christie Tull
Justin Childress
Kay Cattarulla
KMGMT
Olga Kislova

EDITOR'S LEAGUE
Amrit Dhir
Brandon Kennedy
Dallas Sonnier
Garth Hallberg
Greg McConeghy
Linda Nell Evans
Mary Moore Grimaldi
Mike Kaminsky
Patricia Storace
Ryan Todd
Steven Harding
Suejean Kim
Symphonic Source
Wendy Belcher

READER'S LEAGUE
Caitlin Baker
Caroline Casey
Carolyn Mulligan
Chilton Thomson
Cody Cosmic & Jeremy Hays
Jeff Waxman
Joseph Milazzo
Kayla Finstein
Kelly Britson
Kelly & Corby Baxter
Marian Schwartz & Reid Minot
Marlo D. Cruz Pagan
Maryam Baig
Peggy Carr
Susan Ernst

ADDITIONAL DONORS
Alan Shockley
Amanda & Bjorn Beer
Andrew Yorke
Anonymous (10)
Anthony Messenger
Ashley Milne Shadoin
Bob & Katherine Penn
Brandon Childress
Charley Mitcherson
Charley Rejsek
Cheryl Thompson
Chloe Pak
Cone Johnson
CS Maynard
Daniel J. Hale
Daniela Hurezanu
Dori Boone-Costantino
Ed Nawotka
Elizabeth Gillette
Erin Kubatzky
Ester & Matt Harrison
Grace Kenney
Hillary Richards
JJ Italiano
Jeremy Hughes
John Darnielle
Julie Janicke Muhsmann
Kelly Falconer
Laura Thomson
Lea Courington
Leigh Ann Pike
Lowell Frye
Maaza Mengiste

pixel texel

ADDITIONAL DONORS, CONT'D

Mark Haber
Mary Cline
Maynard Thomson
Michael Reklis
Mike Soto
Mokhtar Ramadan
Nikki & Dennis Gibson
Patrick Kukucka
Patrick Kutcher
Rev. Elizabeth & Neil Moseley
Richard Meyer
Scott & Katy Nimmons
Sherry Perry
Sydneyann Binion
Stephen Harding
Stephen Williamson
Susan Carp
Susan Ernst
Theater Jones
Tim Perttula
Tony Thomson

SUBSCRIBERS

Margaret Terwey
Ben Fountain
Gina Rios
Elena Rush
Courtney Sheedy
Caroline West
Brian Bell
Charles Dee Mitchell
Cullen Schaar
Harvey Hix
Jeff Lierly
Elizabeth Simpson
Nicole Yurcaba
Jennifer Owen
Melanie Nicholls
Alan Glazer
Michael Doss
Matt Bucher
Katarzyna Bartoszynska
Michael Binkley
Erin Kubatzky
Martin Piñol
Michael Lighty
Joseph Rebella
Jarratt Willis
Heustis Whiteside
Samuel Herrera
Heidi McElrath
Jeffrey Parker
Carolyn Surbaugh
Stephen Fuller
Kari Mah
Matt Ammon
Elif Ağanoğlu

AVAILABLE NOW FROM DEEP VELLUM

SHANE ANDERSON · *After the Oracle* · USA

MICHÈLE AUDIN · *One Hundred Twenty-One Days* · translated by Christiana Hills · FRANCE

BAE SUAH · *Recitation* · translated by Deborah Smith · SOUTH KOREA

MARIO BELLATIN · *Mrs. Murakami's Garden* · translated by Heather Cleary · *Beauty Salon* · translated by Shook · MEXICO

EDUARDO BERTI · *The Imagined Land* · translated by Charlotte Coombe · ARGENTINA

CARMEN BOULLOSA · *Texas: The Great Theft* · *Before* · *Heavens on Earth* · translated by Samantha Schnee · Peter Bush · Shelby Vincent · MEXICO

MAGDA CARNECI · *FEM* · translated by Sean Cotter · ROMANIA

LEILA S. CHUDORI · *Home* · translated by John H. McGlynn · INDONESIA

MATHILDE CLARK · *Lone Star* · translated by Martin Aitken · DENMARK

SARAH CLEAVE, ed. · *Banthology: Stories from Banned Nations* · IRAN, IRAQ, LIBYA, SOMALIA, SUDAN, SYRIA & YEMEN

LOGEN CURE · *Welcome to Midland: Poems* · USA

ANANDA DEVI · *Eve Out of Her Ruins* · translated by Jeffrey Zuckerman · MAURITIUS

PETER DIMOCK · *Daybook from Sheep Meadow* · USA

CLAUDIA ULLOA DONOSO · *Little Bird*, translated by Lily Meyer · PERU/NORWAY

RADNA FABIAS · *Habitus* · translated by David Colmer · CURAÇAO/NETHERLANDS

ROSS FARRAR · *Ross Sings Cheree & the Animated Dark: Poems* · USA

ALISA GANIEVA · *Bride and Groom* · *The Mountain and the Wall* · translated by Carol Apollonio · RUSSIA

FERNANDA GARCIA LAU · *Out of the Cage* · translated by Will Vanderhyden · ARGENTINA

ANNE GARRÉTA · *Sphinx* · *Not One Day* · *In/concrete* · translated by Emma Ramadan · FRANCE

JÓN GNARR · *The Indian* · *The Pirate* · *The Outlaw* · translated by Lytton Smith · ICELAND

GOETHE · *The Golden Goblet: Selected Poems* · *Faust, Part One* · translated by Zsuzsanna Ozsváth and Frederick Turner · GERMANY

SARA GOUDARZI · *The Almond in the Apricot* · USA

NOEMI JAFFE · *What Are the Blind Men Dreaming?* · translated by Julia Sanches & Ellen Elias-Bursac · BRAZIL

CLAUDIA SALAZAR JIMÉNEZ · *Blood of the Dawn* · translated by Elizabeth Bryer · PERU

PERGENTINO JOSÉ · *Red Ants* · MEXICO

TAISIA KITAISKAIA · *The Nightgown & Other Poems* · USA

SONG LIN · *The Gleaner Song: Selected Poems* · translated by Dong Li · CHINA

JUNG YOUNG MOON · *Seven Samurai Swept Away in a River* · *Vaseline Buddha* · translated by Yewon Jung · SOUTH KOREA

KIM YIDEUM · *Blood Sisters* · translated by Ji yoon Lee · SOUTH KOREA

JOSEFINE KLOUGART · *Of Darkness* · translated by Martin Aitken · DENMARK

YANICK LAHENS · *Moonbath* · translated by Emily Gogolak · HAITI

FOUAD LAROUI · *The Curious Case of Dassoukine's Trousers* · translated by Emma Ramadan · MOROCCO

MARIA GABRIELA LLANSOL · *The Geography of Rebels Trilogy: The Book of Communities; The Remaining Life; In the House of July & August* · translated by Audrey Young · PORTUGAL

PABLO MARTÍN SÁNCHEZ · *The Anarchist Who Shared My Name* · translated by Jeff Diteman · SPAIN

DOROTA MASŁOWSKA · *Honey, I Killed the Cats* · translated by Benjamin Paloff · POLAND

BRICE MATTHIEUSSENT · *Revenge of the Translator* · translated by Emma Ramadan · FRANCE

LINA MERUANE · *Seeing Red* · translated by Megan McDowell · CHILE

ANTONIO MORESCO • *Clandestinity* • translated by Richard Dixon • ITALY

VALÉRIE MRÉJEN · *Black Forest* · translated by Katie Shireen Assef · FRANCE

FISTON MWANZA MUJILA · *Tram 83* · *The River in the Belly: Selected Poems* · translated by Bret Maney DEMOCRATIC REPUBLIC OF CONGO

GORAN PETROVÍC · *At the Lucky Hand, aka The Sixty-Nine Drawers* · translated by Peter Agnone · SERBIA

LUDMILLA PETRUSHEVSKAYA · *The New Adventures of Helen: Magical Tales* · translated by Jane Bugaeva · RUSSIA

ILJA LEONARD PFEIJFFER · *La Superba* · translated by Michele Hutchison · NETHERLANDS

RICARDO PIGLIA · *Target in the Night* · translated by Sergio Waisman · ARGENTINA

SERGIO PITOL · *The Art of Flight* · *The Journey* · *The Magician of Vienna* · *Mephisto's Waltz: Selected Short Stories* · *The Love Parade* · translated by George Henson · MEXICO

JULIE POOLE · *Bright Specimen: Poems from the Texas Herbarium* · USA

EDUARDO RABA[illegible] · *A Zero-Sum Game* · translated by Christina MacSweeney · MEXICO

ZAHIA RAHMANI · *"Muslim": A Novel* · translated by Matthew Reeck · FRANCE/ALGERIA

MANON STEFFAN ROS · *The Blue Book of Nebo* · WALES

JUAN RULFO · *The Golden Cockerel & Other Writings* · translated by Douglas J. Weatherford · MEXICO

ETHAN RUTHERFORD · *Farthest South & Other Stories* · USA

TATIANA RYCKMAN · *Ancestry of Objects* · USA

JIM SCHUTZE · *The Accommodation* · USA

OLEG SENTSOV · *Life Went On Anyway* · translated by Uilleam Blacker · UKRAINE

MIKHAIL SHISHKIN · *Calligraphy Lesson: The Collected Stories* · translated by Marian Schwartz, Leo Shtutin, Mariya Bashkatova, Sylvia Maizell · RUSSIA

ÓFEIGUR SIGURÐSSON · *Öræfi: The Wasteland* · translated by Lytton Smith · ICELAND

DANIEL SIMON, ED. · *Dispatches from the Republic of Letters* · USA

MUSTAFA STITOU · *Two Half Faces* · translated by David Colmer · NETHERLANDS

SOPHIA TERAZAWA · *Winter Phoenix: Testimonies in Verse* · POLAND

MÄRTA TIKKANEN · *The Love Story of the Century* · translated by Stina Katchadourian · SWEDEN

BOB TRAMMELL · *Jack Ruby & the Origins of the Avant-Garde in Dallas & Other Stories* · USA

BENJAMIN VILLEGAS · *ELPASO: A Punk Story* · translated by Jay Noden · MEXICO

SERHIY ZHADAN · *Voroshilovgrad* · translated by Reilly Costigan-Humes & Isaac Wheeler · UKRAINE

FORTHCOMING FROM DEEP VELLUM

MARIO BELLATIN • *Etchapare* • translated by Shook • MEXICO

CAYLIN CARPA-THOMAS • *Iguana Iguana* • USA

MIRCEA CĂRTĂRESCU • *Solenoid* • translated by Sean Cotter • ROMANIA

TIM COURSEY • *Driving Lessons* • USA

ANANDA DEVI • *When the Night Agrees to Speak to Me* • translated by Kazim Ali • MAURITIUS

DHUMKETU • *The Shehnai Virtuoso* • translated by Jenny Bhatt • INDIA

LEYLÂ ERBIL • *A Strange Woman* •
translated by Nermin Menemencioğlu & Amy Marie Spangler • TURKEY

ALLA GORBUNOVA • *It's the End of the World, My Love* •
translated by Elina Alter • RUSSIA

NIVEN GOVINDEN • *Diary of a Film* • GREAT BRITAIN

GYULA JENEI • *Always Different* • translated by Diana Senechal • HUNGARY

DIA JUBAILI • *No Windmills in Basra* • translated by Chip Rosetti • IRAQ

ELENI KEFALA • *Time Stitches* • translated by Peter Constantine • CYPRUS

UZMA ASLAM KHAN • *The Miraculous True History of Nomi Ali* • PAKISTAN

ANDREY KURKOV • *Grey Bees* • translated by Boris Dralyuk • UKRAINE

JORGE ENRIQUE LAGE • *Freeway La Movie* • translated by Lourdes Molina • CUBA

TEDI LÓPEZ MILLS • *The Book of Explanations* • translated by Robin Myers • MEXICO

FISTON MWANZA MUJILA • *The Villain's Dance* •
translated by Roland Glasser • DEMOCRATIC REPUBLIC OF CONGO

N. PRABHAKARAN • *Diary of a Malayali Madman* •
translated by Jayasree Kalathil • INDIA

THOMAS ROSS • *Miss Abracadabra* • USA

IGNACIO RUIZ-PÉREZ • *Isles of Firm Ground* • translated by Mike Soto • MEXICO

LUDMILLA PETRUSHEVSKAYA • *Kidnapped: A Crime Story* •
translated by Marian Schwartz • RUSSIA

NOAH SIMBLIST, ed. • *Tania Bruguera: The Francis Effect* • CUBA

S. YARBERRY • *A Boy in the City* • USA